His broad shoulders strained the limits of his flannel shirt.

And his loose jeans outlined his muscular thighs as he donned protective gloves and hunkered down in front of the cage.

Everything about him was big, including his hands, and yet Emily knew he performed surgery. Strong, yet precise, firm, yet tender… There was no telling what those capable hands would feel like on her bare skin. A shiver of desire passed through her.

She gave herself a mental eye roll and bawled herself out. Now? She was lusting over Seth when the German shepherd was suffering from who knew what? The animals here depended on her to keep them healthy and safe, and find them new homes. They came first. Always.

Seth Pettit was a gorgeous man. He'd also given up his night's rest to help this dog. She'd best get her mind on the matters at hand.

MONTANA VET

BY
ANN ROTH

MILLS
BOON

Ann Roth lives in the greater Seattle area with her husband. After earning an MBA she worked as a banker and corporate trainer. She gave up the corporate life to write, and if they awarded PhDs in writing happily-ever-after stories, she'd surely have one.

Ann loves to hear from readers. You can write her at PO Box 25003, Seattle, WA 98165-1903, USA, or e-mail her at ann@annroth.net.

To animal lovers everywhere

Chapter One

So far, this had been a day of surprises—and not the good kind. Sitting at the front office desk, Emily Miles massaged her temples and thought back to eight o'clock, on what she'd assumed would be a normal Tuesday. She'd assumed wrong.

First Rich Addison, the seventy-something veterinarian who had volunteered at The Wagging Tail since Emily had opened the shelter four years ago, had shared the unwelcome news that he was retiring.

Retiring! The poor man's wife had given him an ultimatum—either leave his career behind and start traveling with her, or live out the rest of his days as a divorced man. His last day was Friday. Emily had no idea where she'd find his replacement, and Rich hadn't come up with any names, either.

On this warm, sunny day in the second week of September—normal weather for Prosperity, Montana—she'd opened all the windows. She easily heard the collective howls and barks coming from the dog runs in the backyard, where the six abandoned and/or abused animals she was sheltering until she found them good homes were enjoying the day as best as they could. At least they had been. The unhappy sounds made her wonder if they somehow understood this dire news and what it meant.

Because without an on-call veterinarian to come in when necessary, she would have no way of knowing if the animals she took in suffered from a contagious disease, or how to treat those in need of medical attention. She would be forced to close down.

Then where would these abandoned, innocent creatures go? To the pound, where they would probably be euthanized. Emily couldn't bear the thought.

An annual fund-raiser brought in enough to keep The Wagging Tail afloat, and Emily counted every penny. As yet, the only two people on the payroll were herself, and she took only enough to cover the rent and supplies, and Mrs. Oakes, the part-time office manager.

As busy as Emily was with the shelter, she also ran a website design and management business from home. The work took up considerable time, but was interesting and covered her personal bills, and sometimes subsidized shortages that fund-raising didn't cover.

But neither her earnings nor the shelter's budget was enough to pay a veterinarian. Someday. For now, she needed a volunteer, preferably long-term. The trouble was, most of the animal doctors in town worked full-time and then some, devoting any spare time to other, larger facilities. Finding someone willing to come to her little shelter without compensation was difficult.

If that wasn't enough, Emily needed him or her by the end of the week—just three days from now.

Could the day get any worse?

It could and had. While she was still reeling from Rich's stunning news, Mrs. Oakes, who worked Tuesday through Friday, had called in sick with a case of stomach flu. Edgar, the senior citizen volunteer who answered the phones on Mondays, had been busy with other commitments, leaving Emily to man the front desk. Then the Tates, the couple scheduled to foster and, fingers crossed, adopt the high-strung red setter that had been at the shelter for nearly a week, had postponed until Friday. With the kennel filled to capacity, Emily had counted on freeing up the dog's cage for another animal in need.

Instead she'd had to turn away two dogs. She'd spent several hours calling everyone she knew, pleading for someone to take in one or both animals. With a lot of begging, she'd finally found them temporary homes. They needed to be seen by a vet, and someone needed to pay for those services.

Her head was pounding now, and her empty stomach was demanding food. With a sigh, she stood and carried her half-empty mug of tepid coffee through the archway off the front office, which had once been a living room. A short walk down the hall led to her small office, formerly a den. There she retrieved her purse from under the desk and dug through it for aspirin. She downed the pills with a healthy slug of the coffee—a combination guaranteed to give her stomach fits if she didn't eat posthaste.

Until now, she hadn't had the time. "I need lunch," she said.

Susannah, the three-legged whippet Emily had taken in and adopted when she'd first opened the shelter, had been napping on the doggy bed in the corner. Now she trotted over—if you could call her odd, limping gait a trot.

Although Emily lived in the apartment upstairs, every morning she stowed a sack lunch in the kitchen on the main floor. Susannah accompanied her there, licking her chops and wagging her tail.

"You already had your meal," Emily said, but the dog knew she was a soft touch.

Moments later, she returned to Mrs. Oakes's desk with the sack lunch and a fresh cup of coffee. Susannah was excited now, yipping and grinning as only she could. "Oh, all right," Emily said. "But first, sit!"

She quickly obeyed. Emily always marveled over that. After all, Susannah had only one front leg. When she'd arrived at the shelter at the age of about one year, she hadn't even been house-trained.

"Good girl," Emily cooed. Reaching into the lunch bag,

she pulled out the dog treat Susannah had known was there. Seconds later, content, the dog settled down on the braided rug nearby.

Emily was munching on her sandwich when the two-way radio buzzed. Caroline, one of the regular volunteers, was out back with the dogs.

"I have to leave soon," she said. "Do you want me to put everyone back in the kennel?"

"They've been out for a while now, and I cleaned their cages and filled their food and water dishes, so yes. Thanks, Caroline—you're the best." Emily meant that. The volunteers who gave so much of their time and effort kept the shelter going.

She finished her lunch, sipping her coffee and culling through applications from the high school kids who wanted to volunteer this semester. Doing so would earn them community-service credit, an annual requirement for students at all four of Prosperity's high schools.

Suddenly Susannah woofed, moved awkwardly to her feet and loped toward the door with her tail wagging. It had taken almost two years of patience and TLC, but she'd finally learned to trust people. The bell over the door jingled.

"Come here." Emily snapped her fingers. The dog obeyed, but wasn't happy about it.

An instant later, a girl entered the office. She looked to be fourteen or so, and was tall and gangly, just as Emily had been at that age. Her shoulder-length, light brown hair had bright red streaks in it, and bangs that same red all but obscured her large eyes. She moved hesitantly toward Emily, her obvious self-consciousness at odds with the sullen look on her face.

It was that contrast that reminded Emily of her own painful adolescent years, as a lonely teen whose mother worked long hours to put a roof over their heads, after Emily's father had left.

"Hi." She smiled. "I'm Emily Miles, the founder of The Wagging Tail."

"Hi." Not even a semblance of a smile.

Susannah jumped up and raced forward with her tail waving. Smiling now, which did wonders for her face, the girl petted the happy canine. "Cool dog. What happened to his leg?"

"Actually, she's female. Her name is Susannah. When she arrived at the shelter, she had a bad infection in her foreleg. We had to amputate."

The girl looked horrified. As if knowing they were talking about her, Susannah woofed softly and retreated to the rug.

"Some of the dogs we take in are in pretty bad shape," Emily said. "But with love, patience and a good home, miracles can happen. I'll bet you're here because you want to do a semester of community service at The Wagging Tail."

The girl's eyes widened in surprise. "How did you know?"

"It's that time of year. I didn't catch your name."

"Taylor."

"Nice to meet you. Which school do you attend?"

"Trenton High."

The school was less than a mile from the shelter. Emily nodded. "Are you a freshman?"

"Sophomore."

"Okay. Do you have any experience with dogs?"

Taylor looked at her as if she were crazy. "I like them."

"Have you ever owned or taken care of one?"

The girl shook her head and crossed her arms. "Why are you asking so many questions? I said I liked them." As in, *Isn't that enough?*

Not exactly the warm and friendly personality Emily wanted at the shelter. Although Taylor had been both with Susannah. As a teen, Emily had never been this sullen, certainly not when she wanted a job.

"I've had a lot of interest from high school kids this semester, and I may be full," she said. Most of them had left any attitude behind and put on their best faces. "But if you'd like to fill out an application, I'll look it over and get back to you."

"You don't want me."

For one telling moment, Taylor's shoulders slumped. Then the surly look reappeared and she raised her head.

Emily guessed that she'd been rejected by someone, somewhere. Having been there herself, when her father had walked out of her life, she sympathized. "I didn't say that," she replied with a smile. "School started in late August, and here we are a few weeks later. Most of the kids who want to work here applied last week." She patted the stack of applications on the desk. "I'm in the process of selecting volunteers now."

"We only moved here a few days before school started. I would've come in sooner, but I just found out about this place."

While it seemed a plausible excuse, Emily wondered if Taylor's attitude had cost her opportunities at other organizations. Wanting to help the girl, she opened a desk drawer and pulled out a blank application. "There's still time to apply." She handed the form over. "Why don't you fill this out?"

"Whatever." The girl stuffed the paper into her backpack. "Where are the other dogs?"

"They spent most of the afternoon out back. Now they're in the kennel—that building over there." Emily pointed at what had once been a large, detached garage. "Would you like to meet them?"

"Uh, yeah." Taylor's snarky tone indicated that this was obvious.

Shaking her head at the girl's hostility, Emily leashed Susannah, then led Taylor down the concrete walkway. The afternoon sun had barely begun its descent toward the horizon, but already the air was noticeably cooler and felt like autumn. In central Montana, the weather was known to change quickly, and in a matter of hours, the temperature could vary by as much as twenty degrees.

Leaving Susannah tethered outside the kennel, Emily opened the door and gestured for Taylor to enter. Harvey, the architect Emily had met when he'd adopted a mixed-breed female from the shelter, and who she'd started dating soon after, had reconfigured the garage into a perfect space to house the dogs. Six large cages were spread across the clean cement floor, each equipped with a dog bed, and food and water bowls. A sink and tub for bathing the animals filled one corner, and a stainless steel exam table took up another, along with shelves and cabinets laden with towels and supplies. One large, airy window flooded the space with light, and good insulation and a heating and cooling system kept the temperature comfortable no matter what the weather.

"As you can see, we're currently filled up," Emily said.

Taylor looked puzzled. "But there are only six dogs here."

"Unfortunately, right now, this is all I have room for. We also have two quarantine huts for when new dogs come in."

Another of Harvey's contributions to the shelter. Emily could actually think about him now without a twinge of the heartbreak she'd suffered when he'd left some fifteen months earlier.

Taylor angled her head and frowned. "Why do you quarantine new dogs?"

"Because they might carry infectious diseases, and we don't want to expose the other animals."

A brown-and-white spaniel-terrier mix whined, and Taylor headed forward.

"Wait," Emily cautioned in a low voice. "He's been abused and could bite you out of fear. To keep him from feeling threatened, lower your eyes and put your knuckles close to the bars so that he can smell you."

Taylor looked taken aback, but complied. After much sniffing and studying her, the dog at last licked her hand through the bars.

"He likes me." She looked pleased. "What's his name?"

"We don't usually name them," Emily explained. "We let the families who adopt them do that."

She checked her watch. The front office had been empty for some minutes now. "I need to get back to the office, in case the phone rings or someone else comes in."

Taylor nodded, and they headed back. As they sauntered down the walkway, the girl's cell phone trilled out bars from some rock song. "If you wanna stick around you gotta cut me some slack," a male voice twanged.

She glanced at the screen and frowned before answering. "Hey, Seth," she said in a bored voice. She listened a moment. "No, I ditched the bus. I'm at The Wagging Tail. The. Wagging. Tail," she repeated, with exaggerated impatience. "It's a dog shelter?" Another silence. "It's for community service. I'm supposed to volunteer, remember? Can you pick me up here?" She listened again. "Yeah, I know I was supposed to call." The irritated breath she blew was loud enough for the person on the other end to hear. "I forgot, okay? Bye." She disconnected.

Talk about unfriendly. She'd been okay with the dogs, but Emily couldn't picture her working at the shelter. Not when Emily had the pick of kids she assumed would be easier to work with. Still, it was only fair to look at her application—provided she turned one in.

"Seth will be here in a little while," Taylor muttered.

"Is he your boyfriend?" If so, the poor boy was a glutton for punishment.

"Boyfriend? Eww." The girl pantomimed sticking her finger down her throat. "Seth is an adult—he's why we moved here."

Ah, so he was Taylor's father. Emily couldn't believe she called him by his first name. This girl was a handful, and Emily felt for the parents. She imagined that if she'd ever called her dad by his first name, she'd have been in major trouble. That is, if he'd stuck around until she hit her teenage years. Since he'd taken off when she was nine, she could only guess.

"Where are you from?" she asked as they entered the front office.

"San Diego."

"That's a big city. Even at the height of tourist season, we only have about seventy thousand residents in Prosperity." Most of the locals were either ranchers or made their living from the tourists, who flocked to the area in late spring and summer for hiking and fishing. And also to visit Prosperity Falls, which was famous for its beauty and a popular place for marriage proposals and weddings. "When the tourists leave, we drop down to sixty thousand," she added. "Is Seth a rancher? Is that why you decided to move here?"

"You ask a lot of questions," Taylor said. "I didn't get a say in whether I moved or not. Otherwise, I would've stayed in San Diego. Seth isn't a rancher, but he used to live here. His brother has a ranch on the other side of town."

Interesting. "What's his profession?"

"He's a veterinarian."

"Is he?" Emily didn't hide her interest. "And his specialty?"

"Large animals."

"You mean livestock?"

Taylor nodded.

"Does he ever treat dogs?"

"Sometimes. When he was at a ranch the other day, he treated a border collie with worms." Taylor shrugged. "While I'm waiting for him, I may as well fill out the application."

Emily handed her a pen. The girl sat down on the old couch that had belonged to Emily's mother before she'd married Bill, around the time Emily had opened The Wagging Tail.

Taylor pulled earbuds and an iPod from a pocket in her backpack and listened to music while she worked on the application.

While Emily sat at the desk, her thoughts whirled. The girl's father was a veterinarian. Maybe he'd be interested in volunteering at The Wagging Tail. Of course, if he did agree to help out, Emily would have to let Taylor do her community service here.

She wasn't thrilled about that, but to bring in a new veterinarian, she could definitely put up with a little attitude.

Some fifteen minutes after Seth Pettit ended the irritating phone call with Taylor, he parked his pickup in the driveway of The Wagging Tail. She tried his patience in every way, but he was determined to bring her around.

The building, a small two-story structure that looked more like a home than an animal shelter, had a big fenced yard and a couple large dog runs.

Seth didn't remember a shelter on this side of town. But then, he hadn't been in Prosperity since just before his eighteenth birthday, some seventeen years ago, when the town had been smaller and less developed.

Back then, he'd been a kid with a huge chip on his shoulder and a penchant for getting into trouble. He'd resented Sly, his big brother, for trying to rein him in, and had all but ignored Dani, their baby sister. One semester short of graduating high school, he'd dropped out instead. Vowing to never return, he'd left Sly and Dani in his dust.

Funny how things changed. Karma was a bitch with sharp claws.

In the almost three weeks since Sly and Taylor had moved here, he'd seen Dani twice and Sly once. The first time the three of them had met after all these years, Seth had dragged Taylor along, Dani had come with her husband, and Sly had brought his wife and two kids. It had been an uncomfortable reunion. Especially with Sly. Dani had quickly forgiven him for staying out of touch all those years. But Sly? Not so much.

Seth's fault, and he meant to fix the rift he'd caused. With barely enough money to tide him and Taylor over for a few months, he also needed to get his business up and running pretty quick. Otherwise they'd have to move out of the two-story house he rented. He wasn't about to let that happen. Taylor had been through a lot and had moved enough, and Seth meant to put down roots right here. The house, a run-down three-bedroom, wasn't exactly top of the line, but it had the potential. Come spring, the landlord planned to sell it. He'd offered Seth first option to purchase, and Seth wanted badly to take him up on it. For Taylor and him, but also to prove to Sly that his screw-up kid brother hadn't turned out so bad, and could be responsible for someone else. He had about six months to save up the down payment.

Last but not least, he had to figure out how to get Taylor to stop hating him. Piece of cake—and the moon was made of sterling silver.

He headed up the cement walkway to the front door, past a black-and-white The Wagging Tail sign decorated with paw prints. The porch, nothing more than a concrete slab, held a welcome mat, and a hand-lettered sign tacked to the door invited him to come inside.

Seth wiped his feet and did just that.

Taylor was sitting on a sagging couch, with a pen in her hand and her head bent over some papers. Surely not homework. Getting her to do that was harder than pulling a decayed tooth from a bad-tempered bull's mouth.

She looked up at him and frowned. "I'm not ready to go yet. I need to fill out this application."

"Hello to you, too," he said. "You're too young to apply for a job."

A look of pure resentment darkened her face. "I *told* you—it's for community service."

There was no point in reminding her that she'd already visited a food bank and a used-clothing collection center and had turned up her nose at both.

But then, she turned up her nose at everything. For some reason, apparently this place was different.

The woman sitting behind the front desk was studying him curiously. She was a real knockout—big eyes, an intriguing mouth and wavy, collar-length blond hair that was tucked behind her ears.

"Hi." She smiled and stood, tall and long-limbed, and rounded the desk. A hot-pink, feminine blouse framed smallish breasts and hips, and faded jeans showcased long, slender legs. She could've been a model.

A three-legged whippet joined her, tail wagging.

"I'm Emily Miles, founder of The Wagging Tail. And this is Susannah." The woman extended her arm.

"Seth Pettit."

They shook hands. Except for a few cursory hugs from Dani, it had been a while since Seth had touched a woman, even in this casual way. Emily had delicate bones and soft, warm skin, and he held on a moment longer than necessary. Blushing, she extracted her hand.

He turned his attention to the dog, letting her sniff his knuckles in greeting. "Hey, there, Susannah."

"Why don't you come into my office and we'll talk while Taylor completes her application," Emily said. "It's right down the hall."

Wondering at that, he shrugged. "Okay. I'll be back shortly," he told Taylor.

She didn't bother to look up from the application. "Whatever." The word seemed to be her mantra.

He followed Emily down a hall, a short distance, but enough for him to check out her fine backside.

She led him to a windowed room just big enough for a desk, two kitchen-style chairs, a bookcase and filing cabinet and a doggy bed. Papers cluttered the desk, along with the usual computer, printer and phone, and a framed photo of an older woman with the same flirty mouth, smiling up at a man with a thick beard and silvery hair, who looked vaguely familiar. Although Seth had no idea why. Emily's parents, he guessed. A clock and a dog calendar adorned one wall, and dark red curtains framed the window. That was about it.

She gestured at the chairs, which were both across from the desk. "Please, sit down."

They took seats, Emily nudging a pile of folders to one side, to make room for a lined yellow pad.

"Taylor tells me that you're a veterinarian and that you're new in town," she said.

"That's right. I'm looking to build my business. If you know of a rancher looking for a vet who makes house calls, I'm your man."

"If you make house calls, then in no time, you'll have more business than you can handle," she said. "How long have you been practicing?"

"Four years now."

Twin lines marred the smooth space between her eyebrows as she moved the pad to her lap and jotted something down. Seth couldn't see what.

"And you specialize in large animals?" she asked.

"Mostly cattle and horses."

"Taylor mentioned dogs."

"Now and then, but I don't have a clinic or an office." At the moment, he couldn't afford either. But someday...

More scribbling.

"What happens if you need a clinic?" she asked.

"I have an agreement with Prosperity Animal Hospital, on the north side of town."

"I know that place." She jotted that down, too.

Weird. It almost felt as if she was interviewing him.

"How does your wife like Prosperity?"

"I'm not married." A couple times he'd come close, but nothing had worked out.

"Oh." Emily brought her hand to her hair and fiddled with it. "I assumed— Never mind. I didn't realize there were any ranches in San Diego."

The comment puzzled him. "I'm sure there are, but I wouldn't know. I've only been there once or twice, and not for long."

Her turn to look confused. "I'm pretty sure Taylor said she was from San Diego."

He nodded. "She is."

"I don't understand. Aren't you her father?"

No one ever understood until he explained. Dani, Sly and their families knew the facts, as did the teachers and counselors at Taylor's school. Now Emily would, too.

"It's complicated," he began, giving her an out if she didn't want to know. She nodded, and he went on. "Taylor's mother and I were involved. We moved in together when Taylor was about five. Four years later, Annabelle broke things off and kicked me out."

She'd stuck with him while he finished college, assuming that eventually they'd marry. Then immediately after earning his undergrad degree, he'd started vet school. Annabelle had continually pushed him to propose, but between school and a part-time job, he'd been too busy to think about much else. That was his excuse, anyway. The truth was he hadn't been ready for marriage. Hell, he'd never even told her he loved her. He'd liked her fine, but hadn't been capable of taking the next step. Tired of waiting for that ring on her finger, Annabelle had ended the relationship.

Story of his life.

"I see." Emily frowned. "If you don't mind my asking, why is Taylor living with you now?"

"I'm getting to that. In the years we lived under the same roof, she and I grew close. Annabelle never knew who Taylor's father was. Although it wasn't me, Taylor considered me to be her father, and I loved her like a daughter.

"At the time, we lived in Sacramento," he went on. "I moved out, and a few days after the breakup, Annabelle packed up and left. She didn't tell me about that or say where she was going, just cut me out of Taylor's life." Not all that different from what Seth had done with Dani and Sly, he'd come to realize a few years later. Standing on the other side of the fence had sucked, big time. "I tried to find them, but never did," he finished.

He'd missed the girl terribly and knew she was likely missing him, too. "Fast-forward six years. I was still in Sacramento, with my own veterinary practice." A few months earlier, his mentor from his undergrad days, Professor Greenfield, had died of cancer. Like Seth, the professor had been estranged from his family. Filled with regret, he'd begged Seth to make up with Sly and Dani before it was too late.

Seth had been mulling that over, assuring himself that he had plenty of time to make amends with his siblings, when the bomb that had radically altered his life had dropped. "Annabelle's attorney contacted me with the news that she'd been in an accident and had passed away," he said. "There was no other family, and in her will, she'd named me to assume guardianship of Taylor."

Annabelle's passing at the young age of thirty-five, the same age Seth was, had added a sense of urgency to make up with Sly and Dani sooner, rather than later. You never knew when your time was up.

"What a shock that must have been for both you and

Taylor," Emily said. "Poor girl. It must be hard to lose your mother at such an early age."

Seth knew way too much about that. He'd lost his own mother when he was ten. Less than a year later, his father had followed her. "I think her death knocked us both to our knees," he said.

As bad as he'd felt for Taylor, at first he'd balked at the idea of assuming responsibility for the girl he hadn't seen in six years. But if he didn't step up, she would go into foster care. Seth couldn't let that happen, couldn't let her go through that.

After both his parents died, Dani had been shuffled into foster care. She'd lucked out, though, when Big Mama, her foster mom, had adopted her. Meanwhile, Seth and Sly had been shipped off to Iowa to live with an uncle who never tired of reminding them that he hated kids. No child deserved to live with a man like that.

"No wonder," Emily murmured.

"Pardon me?"

"Taylor seems to have a bit of an attitude."

And then some. Seth nodded. "The adjustment has been rough on her. On both of us."

He was at his wits' end. In the weeks since they'd moved here, no matter what he did, Taylor had shown nothing but contempt and loathing for both him and Prosperity. She hadn't made a single friend or become involved in any school activities.

This dog shelter was the first thing she'd expressed an interest in. Seth needed Emily to give her a chance. "Be honest with me," he said. "Are you going to let Taylor work here?"

Emily caught her full lower lip between her teeth. "Before we talk about that, I'd like to show you around. It'll only take a few minutes. We'll go out through the front door, so you can let Taylor know. She can stay here and keep Susannah company."

Curious to see the place that had finally piqued Taylor's interest, Seth readily agreed. "Let's go."

Chapter Two

"Tell me about the dogs," Seth said, as Emily led him toward the kennel.

At five feet ten in her bare feet and even taller in boots, she didn't have to look up at people all that often. But Seth was several inches taller, and she had to do just that to meet his eyes. They were an unusual shade of silvery blue, and looked especially striking against the afternoon sky.

"I take in animals that have been abandoned and sometimes abused," she said. "My job is to find them permanent homes with loving families."

He absorbed her words with a somber expression. "You haven't chosen easy work."

"No, but it can be so rewarding."

Seth listened thoughtfully. "Is that how you got Susannah?"

Emily nodded. "She was one of the first dogs to come here when I opened my doors." The whippet, with her injured leg, malnourished body and trembling fear, had quickly wormed her way into Emily's heart.

"How did you get into this work?" Seth asked.

"My very first job was with a woman who groomed and boarded dogs while their owners were out of town," Emily said. She'd taken the job so that she could help her struggling mother make ends meet. "She had a soft place in her heart for abused dogs, and fostered and adopted a few while I worked for her. Like all living creatures, they need love and affection, along with a strong dose of patience. Give them those things, and they're loyal friends for life." Unlike people, who could walk away at any time and break your heart. "I've been in love with dogs ever since."

"Running this place can't be cheap. How do you fund it?"

"Through private donations, most of which I raise at an annual fund-raiser the first Saturday in November," she said. "But I couldn't do it without my volunteers." Mentally, she crossed her fingers that she could persuade Seth to sign on as one of them. "The dog groomer I just told you about? She comes in a couple times a month to bathe and groom the dogs. The rest of the time, I get to do the job." Emily wrinkled her nose.

"I'll bet that gets messy."

He flashed a smile she felt clear to her toes. It had been over a year since she'd even noticed a man, and Seth Pettit was a seriously attractive male, tall and solid, with a broad forehead and a strong jaw. She smiled back. "Even when I wear protective clothing, I usually end up a dripping mess. You don't want to see me when I finish that job."

He chuckled at that, and so did she.

"You do this full-time?" he asked.

She shook her head. "There isn't enough money for that, so I double as a web designer—I create and maintain websites. I enjoy the work, plus I get to set my own hours."

"I've been told I should put up a website, but I'm not sure I need one."

"Can't hurt," Emily said. Wanting Seth to know more about the shelter, she gestured around. "Isn't this a nice space? It used to be part of a ranch that was subdivided and sold off. I rent it from a couple who love animals. They even adopted one of our dogs. They didn't mind when I turned the garage into a kennel. As long as I pay the rent on time, they're happy."

At the kennel, she opened the door and led Seth inside. He moved slowly and deliberately toward the cages, letting the dogs take him in.

"Hey, there," he greeted them.

Each one took note of his low, soothing voice, and a few wagged their tails.

It was obvious that Seth Pettit had a way with animals. Probably with women, too, Emily guessed, with another flutter of interest.

But she wasn't about to see him as anything but a potential volunteer veterinarian at the shelter. Her life was very full and a lot simpler without a man in it, and she liked it that way.

After a moment, they headed outside again. "I'm impressed with what you're doing here, Emily." He held the door open for her. "Now I understand why Taylor wants to work here."

"About that," Emily started, ready to work a deal. It was chilly now, and wishing she'd put on a sweater, she chafed her arms. "Our dogs need friendly, warm volunteers. And Taylor—"

"Hear me out." Seth held his hand palm up, silencing her. "She's not a bad kid. She just needs a little time to get used to all the changes in her life. I'm no therapist, but I know in my gut that doing her community service here would be really good for her. What can I do to convince you to let that happen?"

His eyes pleaded for understanding. He didn't know that he'd provided the perfect segue to the subject Emily wanted to broach. "Funny you should ask," she said. "The vet who has volunteered here since I opened the shelter just retired unexpectedly. I need a replacement."

Seth eyed her. "You're asking me to volunteer at The Wagging Tail."

Crossing her fingers at her sides, she nodded. Only a few yards from the front office now, they stopped to finish the conversation before stepping inside.

"I have an awful lot on my plate right now," he said.

"You're building a practice and settling in. I understand.

I'm not asking you for forty hours a week, or even twenty. I just need someone to perform routine health checkups on any new animals we take in, get them vaccinated, and whatever else they need. And of course, to give them the medical attention they might need if they get injured or sick while they're here."

"How much time are we talking?"

"You saw for yourself that I only have room for six animals. There are also two quarantine huts where new arrivals stay until they're cleared to join the others. Probably one to two hours per week, barring unexpected emergencies."

"So one day a week for two hours?" Seth asked.

"Or more, depending on when we take in a new animal and if someone gets sick. I'll try not to bother you at night or on weekends."

"You'll give Taylor a job if I agree to this?"

Emily nodded.

"Throw in a free website consultation and design and I'll do it. For one semester, while Taylor's here. But understand that if you need me at the same time as someone in my practice, they come first."

A semester was better than nothing. Who knew, maybe she'd convince him to stay on permanently. At the very least, she had a few months to search for someone else.

Relieved, she smiled. "Fair enough. Thank you, Dr. Pettit."

"I go by Seth."

"Okay, Seth. Please call me Emily. Community service begins on Monday."

"Great. Do me a favor, and don't tell Taylor about our arrangement. Let her think she got the job because you want her for herself."

"I can do that," Emily said. "I'll call her tomorrow and let her know."

He nodded. "We have a deal."

They shook on that. Seth's big hand almost engulfed

hers. His grip was firm and strong and warm, and for some reason, Emily wanted to hold on for a while.

Way too attracted to this man, she quickly let go, pivoted away and hurried toward the front door.

"I DON'T SEE why you need to volunteer at The Wagging Tail while I volunteer there," Taylor said as Seth drove home. "That is, if Emily chooses me."

Taylor didn't want him involved in anything she did. In her life at all, for that matter. He stifled a weary sigh. "The vet who was helping Emily retired, and she asked me to help out. I'm only going to do it until January, and my own business comes first. Trust me, I won't get in your way."

Taylor snickered. "You're *always* in my way."

Seth missed the days when she'd been little and carefree, and had simply taken him at his word. But those times were long gone, and a lot of baggage had filled the gap in between. "I'll only come to The Wagging Tail when Emily calls, and if she hires you, to pick you up—that's it," he said, striving to sound patient. At Taylor's stony look he added, "If she doesn't have a vet to handle her dogs' medical issues, she'll be forced to shut down."

Taylor's eyes widened. "I guess it's okay, then."

One hurdle successfully crossed. Relieved, Seth rolled the truck up the cracked blacktop driveway of their house. He pulled into the carport. Before he even killed the engine, Taylor slipped out the passenger door. Without a thanks-for-the-ride or a backward glance, she pulled a house key from her jeans pocket and headed for the house.

Seth followed. As a kid, he'd always been ravenous when he got home from school. He was pretty sure she must be, too. But she went straight through the kitchen and toward the stairs.

Wafer thin, she was way too skinny. He couldn't let her disappear into her room without something to eat. "Hold on," he called out. "Want a snack?"

"No, thanks," she said over her shoulder.

"It's okay to eat in your room or anyplace in the house. It's yours, too. You don't have to hide upstairs."

"I'm not hiding and I'm not hungry."

She spent way too many hours texting and fooling around on FaceTime with her friends in San Diego. Time she should be spending making new friends and getting involved at Trenton High.

But as she continually reminded him, her home was in San Diego and there was nothing for her here. And he reminded her that she lived in Prosperity now. She didn't like that at all.

At least she had her community service work lined up—a first step toward settling in. Seth hoped.

She was almost up the stairs now. "Do your homework before you talk with your friends," he called out.

Muttering, she took the last few steps quickly. Seconds later her bedroom door closed. Loudly.

Seth muttered, too. For his own benefit, he'd talked with a couple specialists about the situation. He wanted Taylor to meet with the school counselor or see a social worker or therapist, but she refused. He knew that he couldn't force her to get help.

He was in his "office," for now a corner of the living room, tackling paperwork and thinking about ways to drum up business, when his cell phone rang.

"This is Zeke Jones," a gravelly voice said. "I got your name from Barton Michaels." Michaels owned a ranch where Seth had treated a sick heifer the previous week, and had gotten Seth's name from an ad he'd placed in the *Prosperity Daily News*. "Got a cow with a bad case of pinkeye," Zeke went on. "It's in both eyes, and I'm worried about it spreading through the herd. She's starting to lose weight, too."

This was not good for Zeke, but Seth was pleased for the referral from Michaels. "Where are you?" he asked.

He jotted down the address. Although it was nearly dinnertime, he said, "I'll be over shortly."

After disconnecting, he headed upstairs to tell Taylor.
Maybe she'd come with him. Through the door he heard
loud music from The Wanted, a band she listened to con-
stantly. He knocked a couple times before she heard him.

"What do you want?" she asked through the closed door.

"Open up."

Seconds later, the door opened a fraction, just enough
for her to poke her head through.

"I have to go out and help a rancher with a cow who
has pinkeye," he said, raising his voice above the music.

"Whatever." She started to close the door.

"Why don't you come along?" he asked. "It's bound to
be interesting." And might help them bond.

She looked as if she'd rather eat worms. "What's interesting about pinkeye?"

"In a cow, it can be dangerous. It hurts a lot more than it
does in humans. An infected animal often keeps her eyes
closed because of the pain. She avoids sunlight, too, and
stops foraging for food and water. If she doesn't get well
quickly, she could die."

"That's not interesting at all."

The door shut rudely in his face. Patience fraying, he
bit back a frustrated oath. When he was in vet school,
she'd loved watching him work with sick or injured animals. Not anymore. Since he'd taken Taylor in and they'd
moved here, he'd made sure to invite her along on any call
he made when she wasn't in school. So far, she'd always
turned him down.

"I should be back in an hour or so, but I'll phone when
I know for sure," he said through the door. No reply. "If
you want dinner while I'm gone, there's leftover lasagna
in the fridge," he added.

Nothing but hostile silence.

His fraying patience snapped. This time he opened the door without knocking. "Did you hear what I said?"

"I didn't say you could come in here." Arms crossed, Taylor shot daggers out of her eyes.

"Tough. Did you hear me or not?"

"I heard."

Seth nodded. "See you later. Get that homework done before you start texting or using FaceTime."

"Yes, sir." Sarcasm dripped from her words.

When he was through the door, she slammed it.

Irritated at himself for losing his cool, he scrubbed his hand over his face and headed back down the stairs. Living in the same house with an angry teenage girl was a lot tougher than he'd ever imagined.

Would she ever give him a break?

AFTER LOCKING THE shelter doors late Thursday afternoon, Emily drove toward Prosperity Park. Her mother and Bill lived on the edge of the park, and were lucky enough to have an impressive view of Prosperity Falls from their living room window. A view that had cost a bundle, but Bill was a partner in a large insurance company and could afford it.

He gave Emily's mother whatever she wanted, and she wanted to travel. In two days, they would leave for six whole weeks, touring Spain, Portugal and France.

Emily was jealous, but in a good way. If she didn't have the time or money to travel, at least they did. Tonight they'd invited her over for dinner and to say goodbye.

The sun was about to set and vivid pink streaks colored the paling sky. The usual rush-hour traffic filled the highway, but Emily didn't mind. With beauty all around her and dinner plans, she couldn't help but be happy.

Too happy for a ho-hum night with her mom and Bill. She really needed to get out more.

She parked in the driveway of the house, which was a

stunning mixture of cream-colored brick, river stone and tempered glass. The landscaped yard was nothing like the trampled grass around the shelter grounds. Carrying a bottle of Spanish wine she'd picked up, she followed the flagstone walkway to the raised brick stoop, then opened the front door and let herself in.

The place was quiet. Leaving her jacket and purse in the entry, Emily headed for the living room, on the opposite side of the house. The huge space was only marginally smaller than her entire apartment, and decorated with beautiful, expensive furnishings.

Where were her mother and Bill? After stopping to admire the falls from the picture window, Emily checked the state-of-the-art kitchen. No one there, either. She peered out the sliding glass door that opened onto the back yard and patio. The grill was out and ready for action, but she didn't see her mother or stepfather.

She set the wine she'd brought on the granite counter and returned to the living room. "Hello?" she called. "Mom? Bill? I'm here!"

"We'll be right out!" Her mother's muffled reply came from the direction of the master bedroom.

A long few minutes later, the couple appeared, with their arms around each other's waists. Her mother looked slightly disheveled and radiant, and Bill wore a big grin. Emily didn't want to think of what had put the glow in their faces. Some things were too gross to contemplate. Four years of marriage and they still acted like newlyweds.

They were insanely happy, which was wonderful. After Emily's father had walked out and left her mom struggling to pay the bills and keep a roof over their heads, she deserved a loving man. She liked to say that Bill's wealth was the icing on her happiness cake.

Emily didn't care about Bill's money. He was a good guy who really cared about her mother. She wanted a man like Bill. She'd thought she'd found him in Harvey. They'd discussed marriage and children multiple times, and she'd assumed that they would be together forever.

Then a well-known architecture firm on the East Coast had offered him a plum job. Emily hadn't wanted to give up her beloved shelter, but she'd been ready to find her replacement so that she could go with him. Things hadn't worked out the way she'd imagined, however. Harvey had taken his dog with him, but not Emily. She'd been single ever since.

Her mother came over to exchange cheek kisses with her. Bill gave her a hug.

"How's the packing coming along?" she asked.

"We were just working on that, only then we got a little distracted." Her mother and Bill exchanged meaningful glances.

He chuckled. "We sure did."

TMI—too much information, Emily thought. She cleared her throat. "I noticed you uncovered the grill out back."

"We're having steak tonight." Bill licked his lips and patted his slight paunch. "Are you hungry, Em?"

"Starving."

"Me, too. As soon as I fix the drinks, I'll fix the steaks."

In the kitchen, Emily's mother and Bill kissed as if they were about to part for days before he stepped through the sliding glass door to the patio.

Her mother watched him go with a dreamy sigh. Emily shook her head. Sometimes the lovey-dovey stuff got old. "What can I do to help?" she asked.

"Set the table and open that bottle of wine so it can breathe. I'll heat the rolls and empty the salad into a bowl."

While they worked, they caught up on each other's lives, just as they had when they'd lived in the one-bedroom apartment where Emily had grown up—on the rare occasions when her mother had been home in time to help with the evening meal. Usually, Emily had prepared it alone.

Before long, Bill returned with the sizzling steaks. They sat at the kitchen table and loaded their plates.

"Are you excited about your trip?" Emily asked as they ate.

"Just a little." Bill's lips twitched.

He and Emily's suddenly gleeful mother exchanged brilliant grins, and then launched into a detailed itinerary of where they were going and when. Emily had already heard most of before, but didn't mind hearing it again. In their excitement, the two finished each other's sentences and occasionally interrupted one another. They were so involved in the back and forth that they seemed to forget she was there.

Emily felt like a third wheel. Melancholy crept in, and no longer hungry, she picked at her food. At times like this, she wished she was part of a couple.

But that would mean dating again, which she hadn't done since Harvey. Emily's wayward thoughts homed in on a certain sexy veterinarian. She quickly dismissed that idea. She'd had to resort to arm twisting to get Seth to take the volunteer job in the first place, and she wasn't about to jeopardize that by going out with the man. If he was even interested. Because if they were to go out and then things between them soured... At any time, he could walk away from the shelter. Besides, between it and her website business, she was way too busy to date.

Which wasn't exactly the full truth. The thing was, even though it had been more than fifteen months since Harvey had left, and even though Emily was totally over him, she wasn't over what he'd done. Bad enough, breaking her heart. He wasn't the first. But leaving her behind without a backward glance, the same as her father had? She wasn't about to put herself in that position ever again, and she for sure wasn't ready to start dating. Besides, the dogs at the shelter depended on her, and that was where her focus needed to be—on providing them with a temporary place to stay and finding them good homes.

Refusing to be ignored for one more minute, she changed the subject. "I had an unpleasant surprise this week." That got her mother and Bill's attention. "You remember Rich Addison, the veterinarian who's volunteered at the shelter since I opened our doors? He decided to retire."

Knowing what that meant, her mother frowned. "What are you going to do?"

"I think I've found a replacement."

"Already? That's great!" Bill looked pensive. "I've sold insurance policies to most of the animal docs in town. Who is it?"

"Actually, he's new here, having recently moved back from California. His name is Seth Pettit and he works mostly with livestock."

"I know Seth." Bill nodded. "He phoned shortly after he arrived, and I set him up with the insurance he needs."

Her mother frowned. "If Dr. Pettit works with livestock, why is he volunteering at the shelter?"

"He likes to be called by his first name," Emily said. "His..." She paused. How to explain Taylor? "He's guardian to a teenage girl who will be doing her community service at The Wagging Tail."

"They're volunteering together." Bill gave a nod of approval. "I used to do that with Kara." His daughter from his first marriage, now in her early forties. "It's a good bonding experience."

"They won't exactly be doing their volunteer work at the same time," Emily said.

"Still, it's nice that they'll both become familiar with the shelter. They'll have something to talk about."

She hadn't thought of it that way, but Bill was right.

They were finishing their dessert when her "dog emergency" pager buzzed. The number of one of the volunteers who rescued abused animals showed on the screen. "I need to check this," Emily said. "Excuse me."

She stepped into the hallway and returned the call. Moments later, she reentered the kitchen. "Sorry to eat and run, but a new dog is coming in tonight, and I have to make some calls."

First, to the couple who'd said they wanted the red setter, to make sure they picked him up in the morning, which would free up a slot for the new animal. Then, to Seth Pettit. Tonight she would quarantine the new arrival. Depending on what Seth found when he examined the dog, the animal would either move in with the others or stay in quarantine.

Chewing a bakery cupcake, her mother nodded.

"That's okay, Em," Bill said. "Between packing and other things, your mother and I have plenty to keep us busy."

Once again, they exchanged a private, loving look. *Brother.*

Emily kissed and hugged them both. "I'll miss you two," she said. "Call and email when you can—and send pictures."

"We will," her mother said. "Good luck with the new vet. And the new dog."

Before Emily even reached her car, she'd pulled out her phone.

Chapter Three

"Can I come with you to The Wagging Tail today?" Taylor asked Seth over breakfast Friday morning. They were sitting in the nook off the kitchen.

Since they'd moved here, this was a first. She'd never asked to go on a call, and for a moment, Seth wondered if she was finally accepting him and settling into her new life. Then his natural cynicism kicked in. Did she really want to watch him examine the shelter's newest dog, or was this a ploy to get out of going to school? Likely the latter.

"If it wasn't a school day, you could," he said, "but I don't want you missing any classes."

His own words took him aback. Damned if he didn't sound just like Sly had all those years ago, whenever Seth had tried to weasel his way out of going to school.

Would wonders never cease.

Taylor's dirty look told him he'd guessed right. "I hate you and I hate Prosperity!"

Seth winced, but he'd heard it before, more times than he could count. You'd think he'd be used to that, but every time she used the *H* word, it stung. He'd be damned if he'd let on how badly. "Look," he said. "You'll probably see the dog Monday, when you go to the shelter for orientation."

One skinny shoulder lifted, then dropped. She turned away from him and stared out the window that faced the raggedy backyard—who had time for yard work?—and the house behind them. The leaves on the trees scattered around the yard were starting to turn. Seth hadn't lived through an autumn in Montana for a long time, but he remembered the intense reds and yellows that dressed up the landscape. He also remembered how quickly the weather could turn. Almost as quickly as Taylor's moods.

In the tense silence he'd grown used to, he scraped the last of his Wheaties from his bowl and finished his coffee. After he and Taylor had been reunited, he'd tried hard to ease the transition by talking about his own life and asking questions about hers. When that had failed, he'd offered to take her to a movie or a concert of her choice here in Prosperity, or to drive her and any friends she made.

No luck with that, either. She'd turned him down and tuned him out. Out of sheer desperation, he'd asked her what *did* she want. She had a ready answer for that. She wanted him to take her back to San Diego, drop her off and let her live her life without him in it. Ouch.

If only she'd make friends at school. Even one would help. As far as Seth knew, it hadn't happened. Taylor went to school downcast, and came home with the same dark cloud over her head. They'd been in Prosperity almost a month now, and he still had no idea how to help her adjust. Since she wouldn't talk to a professional, he could only wait for her to settle in and accept that this was her new life.

The way things stood right now, he wondered if she ever would.

"It's almost time for you to catch the bus," he said. "I'm not sure when I'll be home. After I leave The Wagging Tail, I have appointments at two ranches on opposite sides of town. One with a sick bull, and the other with a horse that won't eat. Call me when you get home this afternoon."

Taylor barely nodded.

Shortly after she trudged to the school bus and boarded—would she ever walk like a carefree teenage girl?—he grabbed his doctor bag, hopped into the pickup and headed for Emily's.

The sun was already bright, with the Cascade Mountains in sharp relief against the clear blue sky. Today would be warm, more like summer than fall. That and a couple of paying appointments on the schedule boosted his spirits. Whistling softly, he cracked the window and slipped on his sunglasses.

He looked forward to seeing Emily this morning. He wouldn't mind getting to know her…

As if he had time for that. Building his business, making amends with his brother and dealing with Taylor took up every minute—and then some.

She probably had a boyfriend, anyway. A beautiful woman like her would.

But if she didn't?

Seth didn't exactly have a good track record with women. With relationships, period. He wasn't about to wreck Taylor's community-service experience by getting involved with the woman who'd hired her. Because if he and Emily did get involved, it wouldn't last. It never did.

He was almost at The Wagging Tail. Pushing his wayward thoughts aside, he signaled, slowed and turned into the driveway.

STANDING AT HER kitchen window Friday morning, which was directly above the shelter and faced the front door, Emily peered anxiously through the curtains. The dog that had arrived last night was skin and bones, with what looked like a bad case of mange, and she was anxious for Seth to check her out and put her on the road to a clean bill of health. He was due at eight, a few minutes from now.

Emily didn't usually start the coffee downstairs until closer to nine, but today she went down and started it early, in case Seth wanted a cup. Then she returned to her apartment to make her lunch.

She was sliding her sandwich into a plastic bag when she heard a truck trundle up the driveway. Right on time. When she peered out the window, Seth's dark green pickup was braking to a stop. He didn't glance up, giving her the opportunity to study him openly. In loose, slightly faded jeans, cowboy boots and a long-sleeved blue twill shirt that emphasized his broad shoulders, he looked good. Really good.

Her heart lifted, and not just because she needed his veterinary skills. He pulled a medical bag and a lab coat from the truck.

For the second time in thirty minutes, she hurried down the stairs, answering the door before he knocked.

Seth looked surprised, his startling, silvery-blue eyes widening. "Am I late?"

Emily's cheeks warmed. She wasn't sure why she was blushing. Maybe it was the intensity of his expression. "You're right on time," she said. "It's just...I'm anxious about this dog. Thanks for making us your first appointment of the day."

"This time fits easiest with my schedule."

"Would you like some coffee?"

"No, thanks. Let's take a look at the new arrival."

Leaving the door unlocked for Mrs. Oakes, Emily headed with Seth for the quarantine hut.

"Tell me about her," he said on the way.

"She's a mixed breed, about the size of a retriever, with thick fur. She has mange."

He nodded. "Where did she come from? Did you check for a microchip?"

"Two of my volunteers found her wandering along Ames River. She's pretty scared and full of fight, but working together, they were able to get her into their truck and bring her here. We didn't find a tag or microchip, but just in case, we're posting Lost Dog signs all over the area." Emily didn't expect a response. "I'm pretty sure she's been abandoned, and by the looks of her, she's been on her own for a while."

"Has she had any water or eaten anything since you took her in?" Seth asked.

"Water and a little food last night, and again about an hour ago." Emily had slipped a long-handled spatula through the food gate to deliver this morning's nourishment. "Her belly is distended, and I know that feeding her too much, too quickly, could cause her intestines to twist."

"Right." Seth looked impressed. "Is your friend who bathes the dogs coming in this week?"

Emily shook her head. "I'll be doing the job myself, after you check her over."

In the small quarantine hut, Seth looked even bigger. He donned the lab coat, probably to protect his clothing. As they approached the animal, she scrambled to the back corner of the cage, growling and baring her teeth. Emily hated that the dog was afraid. No, she wasn't just afraid, she was terrified. Her thick coat was matted, with an ugly bald patch on one side. It hurt to look at her.

"Stay back here," Seth ordered under his breath.

Emily nodded and he slowly neared the cage, with his eyes lowered and his body turned sideways to minimize any perceived threat to the animal.

"Hey, there, girl," he murmured in a deep, friendly voice that flowed over Emily and took all her worries away. The man could make a fortune using that voice as a relaxation specialist.

When the dog continued to growl and bare her teeth, Seth froze, but continued to speak softly and without any trace of fear. Long minutes later, the growling stopped and the dog dropped her threatening stance. Seth carefully extended his arm so that his hand almost touched the cage, with his knuckles facing the canine. All the while, he continued to talk to her. After a long time, she inched closer and sniffed him through the wire.

When that seemed to go well, Seth calmly extracted a dog biscuit from his lab coat pocket and dropped it through the bars. The hungry female snatched the treat and inhaled it.

"Good girl," he crooned.

Oh, that voice. As seductive and rich as dark chocolate, it washed over Emily. The dog wasn't nearly as enamored, but she did seem less wary.

"You're really good with her," Emily said in a low voice that wouldn't upset the animal. "Do you want to muzzle her during the exam?"

"I think I'd better."

Emily pulled the device from a shelf against the wall and handed it to Seth. After donning protective gloves, he unlatched the cage door. Before the canine knew what he was up to, he'd slipped the muzzle over her mouth and fastened the straps. She didn't like that at all, but Seth continued to speak in a reassuring voice. When she calmed a little, he brought her out.

Emily was impressed. She slipped into the smock she kept on a hook, and pulled on rubber gloves. While Seth examined the dog and administered the needed vaccines, she cleaned the cage, replaced the dirty bedding and filled the bowl with fresh water.

Then she joined Seth at the exam table.

"She's malnourished, but seems to be in reasonably good health, considering. It's obvious that she's had pups, but I'm not sure if she's been spayed. Can you hold her while I shave her belly and check for a scar?"

Emily nodded. She held tightly to the dog while Seth did what he needed to. The poor thing was shivering with fear.

All the while, Seth spoke reassuringly. "You've been spayed and that's real good. Emily, keep hold of her while I can check her teeth and gums."

While Emily continued to restrain the animal, Seth removed the muzzle. "We won't get the test results until Monday or Tuesday," he said as he worked. "Meanwhile, I want you to give her an antiparasitic medication for the mange. I have enough for two doses with me, and a sample vial of a flea shampoo that will help with her secondary skin infection. You'll need more of both. When we finish here, tell me which pharmacy you use and I'll phone in the prescriptions."

"How long should I keep her in quarantine?" Emily asked.

"Mange can be contagious, so keep her away from the others until it clears up. That could take a while. Hold tight to her a little longer."

He rifled through his medical bag until he found what he was looking for. "Hide this pill in some wet dog food, and it should go down easy. Let's get her bathed."

"That's not part of your job description," Emily said. "Besides, I'm a pro. I've been bathing dogs for ages."

"I don't doubt that, but this one has a lot of fur and she's frightened. I'll give you a hand, just this once."

Grateful for the help, Emily accepted the offer. "Are you sure you have time?"

Seth checked his watch. "I do if we get the job done in under twenty minutes. Where do you want to do this?"

"It's nice today. How about outside."

Seth nodded and glanced around the little hut. "Is that a dog tub in the corner?"

"It is."

After adding shampoo, a sponge and several towels to the heavy tub, Emily dragged it toward the door. Seth re-fastened the muzzle on the dog, slipped a leash around her neck and followed.

This morning, autumn seemed months away. Birds chirped happily and the air was warm. Squinting against the light, Emily zipped up her smock.

The dog fought her bath with everything she had, and despite the protective smock, Emily was soon soaked through. Ten minutes later, the animal was shampooed and rinsed, toweled dry and back in her clean cage.

Emily removed the useless smock. Even her head was wet. Seth's, too. His short, dark brown hair looked almost black, and drops of water glistened like crystals. When he removed his sodden lab coat, she saw that he was every bit as wet as she was.

"We both look like drowned rats," she said, laughing.

Shaking his head and chuckling, he grabbed two towels from the dwindling stack on the shelf and tossed one to her.

Watching him towel off, even fully clothed, was mesmerizing. His wet shirt clung to his flat belly, and the muscles in his arms flexed while he rubbed the water from his hair. He caught her gaping at him. His eyes warmed and a smile hovered around his mouth.

Her face hot, Emily put the bath supplies away. Seth hunkered down in front of the dog's cage, where the newcomer was devouring half a bowl of food with the pill embedded.

"Feeling better, huh, girl?" he asked, when she finished the meal.

The dog angled her head at Seth, then, to Emily's amazement, licked his hand.

After spending less than an hour with him, some of it in a bath, no less, she'd decided to trust him.

Emily was impressed, and if she were honest with herself, just as smitten. Clearly, Seth understood and liked dogs, which elevated him ten notches on her admiration scale. She could so develop a crush on this man—if she was in the market. Which she wasn't.

"What kind of dog do you have, Seth?" she asked.

"None right now. A couple months before I moved back here, Rollie, my black lab, died of old age."

"Why don't you get another one?" she asked, stuffing her smock and the wet towels into a plastic bag to be laundered. "Would you like me to wash your lab coat?"

"No, thanks. I'll get a new dog when life settles down and I have time." He put the muzzle away. "At the moment, my hands are full—both with getting the business going and with Taylor." A pained expression crossed his face.

"Is everything okay?" Emily asked.

"I wouldn't know." He balled up his wet lab coat. "She only speaks to me when she has to, and then it's one or two words. This morning, she almost bit my head off. She wanted to come with me, but I made her go to school instead. Now I'm regretting that. This would've been just as educational."

"You can bring her with you another time. I'm sorry she's so difficult."

"Hey, it's not your problem."

No, but Emily wished she could help. "When you and Taylor are ready for a new dog, don't forget The Wagging Tail," she said.

"I won't." He checked his watch. "I should go."

She nodded and they left the quarantine hut.

As EMILY SAUNTERED beside Seth toward his pickup, he tried hard to keep his eyes off her chest and on her face. Trouble was, her off-white blouse was wet and almost transparent. He could see the pink lace on her bra, and her rosy, perky nipples.

A certain part of him woke up and stirred. He willed his body to behave.

As his renegade eyes darted to her breasts again, she glanced down at herself. Blushing, she hugged the bag of wet towels to her chest.

They were a few yards from the truck when a silver Ford sedan pulled up. A plump, fifty-something woman exited the car.

"That's Mrs. Oakes," Emily said. "She manages the office."

"Good morning, Emily," the woman said with a curious look. "Who's this?"

"Mrs. Oakes, meet Dr. Seth Pettit, our new vet."

Seth flashed a smile. "Nice to meet you."

"And you, as well." She fluttered lashes thick with mascara. "Welcome to our little corner of making the world a better place. By the look of you both, I can see that we've taken in a new dog who didn't care for his bath."

Seth glanced down at his wet shirt and realized he looked like he'd been hit with a water balloon. He was just as soaked as Emily, but on her, wet looked seriously good.

Emily nodded. "She has mange and God knows what else. For now, she'll be staying in quarantine. Oh, and the Tatse should be here this morning to take the red setter."

"It's about time. I'll keep an eye out for them." Mrs. Oakes gave Seth a warm smile before aiming a sly look at Emily. "Emily could toss that shirt in the dryer for you, and give you a cup of coffee while you wait for it."

Both sounded good, but he'd already been there longer than planned. "I appreciate the offer, but I need to go. Nice meeting you, Mrs. Oakes."

"You, as well. I look forward to your next visit, and I'm sure Emily does, too." With a flirty toss of her short brown hair, she sashayed toward the building and disappeared inside.

"Was she flirting with me, or trying to push you and me together?" he asked, shaking his head.

"Both. Her husband left her last year, and she's hungry to meet a new one."

Seth chuckled. "Besides the fact that I'm about twenty years too young for her, I have too much on my plate to date right now. Why would she want to push us together?"

"Because she thinks I should get married." Emily rolled her eyes.

"You're single, then?"

"Yes, and I like it that way."

Seth absorbed this with interest. He wondered why she preferred to be alone. Not that her love life was any of his business. "I can't believe a woman like you isn't with someone," he said.

"A woman like me?" She looked puzzled.

"You're beautiful, smart and passionate about your work. Any man would be lucky to be with you."

Another telltale blush colored her face. "I am dedicated," she agreed, brushing off the compliments.

Making him wonder again. Did she not realize how extraordinary she was? He barely knew her, but he knew enough to appreciate her commitment and passion for the animals she cared for.

"So you're not dating anyone?" he asked, because he wanted to know.

"Between running the shelter and managing my web business, I don't have time."

Her eyes were a pretty light blue, the same color as the early morning sky. A man could get lost in them. "Lack of time—something we have in common," he said, and to his own ears his voice sounded a shade huskier than normal.

She hugged the bag of wet towels closer. "Tell Taylor that I look forward to seeing her on Monday."

"Will do. I hope she behaves herself. By then, I should have the results of the dog's blood work. Before I forget, I need your pharmacy information."

Pulling her phone from her hip pocket, Emily found the number and gave it to him. "Thanks again for making this your first stop of the day," she said.

"No problem." With her helping, he'd actually enjoyed examining and bathing the squirmy, scrawny mutt. "I'll phone in those prescriptions right away. You have your work cut out for you with that dog."

"I'm used to it. Bye for now." She extended her arm, all businesslike.

Touching her was every bit as electric as the other times they'd shaken hands. By the flush in her cheeks and the darkening of her pupils, Seth knew that she felt the same powerful awareness.

He glanced at her mouth again. The cleft in the center

of her top lip begged him to taste it, and that plump lower lip… Suddenly he wanted to kiss her. Badly.

The responding desire in her eyes was irresistible.

He reached for her, but she shot a nervous glance at the big window of the front office. "Mrs. Oakes is probably watching us. She's a big gossip."

"Noted." He pulled Emily around the side of the house, out of view. "Now we're safe," he murmured, caressing her soft, soft cheek.

She didn't answer, but her eyelids lowered a fraction. When he leaned in for the kiss, she stopped him.

"No," she said, stepping back out of reach. "Don't."

Despite the *kiss me* signals from her, she'd changed her mind. Feeling both disappointed and relieved, he gave a terse nod. "I'll, uh, see you Monday."

Seth climbed into his truck and drove away.

Chapter Four

By two o'clock Monday, Emily was ready to begin the orientation for the eight fifteen- and sixteen-year-old community-service volunteers.

They began to trickle in to the shelter. First a girl from Jupiter High, a school on the south side of town. Then a boy and girl from Merrybrook, the high school in the wealthiest part of Prosperity. The rest, a girl and three boys, hailed from Trenton, the school Taylor attended.

Except for Taylor, the Trenton kids entered the building together. Minutes later, she wandered in alone. She barely acknowledged the others from her school, and vice versa. Were they excluding her because they were juniors and she was a sophomore, or for some other reason?

Emily remembered her own teen years, wanting so badly to fit in and be liked. She hadn't exactly been popular, but she'd known she could count on the few friends she'd had. She hoped Taylor would be as lucky.

She passed around the name tags she'd made. "Welcome to The Wagging Tail orientation," she said. "Let's start by introducing ourselves."

After the introductions, Matt from Merrybrook posed a question. "This is a small shelter. How are you going to find enough for all of us to do?"

"Good question. To answer that, let's take a tour of the place. You've all seen the kennel, and we'll visit it again today, but there's a lot more. While I show you around, I'll explain what you'll be doing."

She led them through the main floor of the house, pointing out her office, the supply closets and the kitchen. Outside, they visited the dog runs, and finally, the quarantine hut that housed the dog Seth had examined. The other hut stood empty.

"What's wrong with him?" asked Cat, the only student from Jupiter High.

"She's a female," Emily corrected. "She has mange and worms, but our veterinarian, Dr. Pettit—oops, he prefers to be addressed as Seth—assures me that she'll be okay. Speaking of Seth, Taylor, would you mind if I mentioned your connection to him?"

The girl glanced down. "We don't have a connection," she muttered. "Except that I'm stuck living at his house."

"This dog arrived Thursday night," Emily went on. "After Seth examined her Friday morning, he sent her blood and stool samples to the lab."

She hadn't stopped thinking about his gentle ways with the dog, or the fact that she'd almost kissed him. Her strong desire and feelings for him had startled her. Why him, and why now?

Maybe it was time.

But did she really want a distraction she didn't need in her life right now? No, she told herself. She didn't.

"Earlier, Seth called with some good news," Emily said. "Other than mange and worms, this dog is healthy. Considering that she was starving when she was picked up, and had probably been living on the streets for a while, that's great news."

"If she's healthy, why does she have to stay here by herself?" Cat asked.

"Because both mange and worms are contagious. She's on medicine, and I'm bathing her with a special shampoo. The worms will be gone quickly, but curing the mange will take longer. She's still available for adoption, but until her skin is cleared up, I can't move her into the kennel."

"You mean these dogs get *adopted*?" Cat asked. "I'm adopted."

"That's interesting, Cat. I'm just as careful finding a stable home for our dogs as a human adoption agency is finding a good home for children. Anyone interested in adopting one of our dogs must fill in a detailed application and meet with me, both here at the shelter and in their home."

All the teens seemed impressed.

The tour ended in the kitchen, which was the best place to gather a group. The teens crowded around the kitchen table. Emily stood in front of them. "There are a couple more things to discuss," she said. "First, keeping this shelter open costs money. Besides rent, dog food and supplies, I pay a part-time office manager. You'll meet her next time."

"Don't forget Seth," commented Birch, one of the boys from Taylor's school.

"Actually, we're fortunate that he's volunteering his services. People always want to know where I get the funds to keep this place running. The money comes mostly from private donations. Every year, in early November, I host a fund-raiser. This year, you and your families are all invited. You're also going to play a big part in the event. Which brings me to the brainstorming party I'm hosting for our fund-raiser, two weeks from Friday, in my apartment, which is upstairs in this building." Emily gestured in the direction of the staircase.

"I'd like you all to come, so please write down the date or put it in your phone. We'll have pizza from Harper's Pizza, and I'll be asking for your ideas."

They gave her blank looks, so she explained. "For example, last year, we hosted a dinner and raffle at the Bitter & Sweet downtown. People bought raffle tickets for a chance to win various prizes. They also donated money. That night, we took in enough to stay open one more year."

"Cool," Cat said.

"It's very cool," Emily agreed. "So be thinking about ideas for that."

"What if we have to work or there's a football game?" Shayna from Merrybrook asked. "I'm on the cheer squad and I can't miss the game. Same with Matt—he's on the football team."

"Come for an hour, then, but if you can't, you can't," Emily said. "Now it's time to figure out who you want to do your community service with, and which day you would like to volunteer. Since there are eight of you, and community service days are Monday through Thursday, you'll work in teams of two."

Matt exchanged confused looks with Shayna. "You aren't going to assign us?"

Emily shook her head. "I'm leaving that up to you. Keep in mind that it's always good to make a new friend from a different school. Feel free to get up and walk around and get to know each other. I'll give you a few minutes."

Standing out of the way, she watched the teens pair up. Most of them stuck with kids from their own school. But there were five from Trenton, and Taylor ended up the odd person out. Cat was also alone.

From across the kitchen, the two girls eyed each other. Appearance-wise, they were polar opposites. Cat was petite and curvy. About five feet two, she wore dark eye makeup and her dyed-black hair was boyishly short. A crop top hugged her torso, and under a flouncy, tie-dyed skirt she wore blue tights and black ankle boosts. Taylor was about Emily's height, and willowy, her long red bangs all but hiding eyes with far less makeup. She was dressed in a sleeveless, hooded knit tank top that covered her boyish hips, tight jeans and TOMS flats.

Cat moved first, heading toward her. "It looks like we're the only two left," she said. "Do you want to work together?"

Her expression impassive, Taylor shrugged. "Guess so."

Emily moved to the white board attached to the wall and clapped her hands for attention. "Now that everyone has a partner, let's figure out who comes on what days. Then you can go home, and those who choose Tuesday, Wednesday or Thursday can come back later this week."

What should have been a simple process took almost thirty minutes, but at last everyone was satisfied.

Taylor and Cat had chosen Thursdays. They parted without saying much to each other. Emily hoped they would become friends. She didn't know about Cat, but Taylor could use one.

WHEN SETH PARKED in front of The Wagging Tail after orientation, Taylor was outside, waiting for him. He didn't see Emily or any of the other kids.

"Hey," he said, sliding out to greet her.

Wearing her trademark earbuds, her head moving to the beat of whatever song she was listening to, she barely glanced up from her phone to acknowledge him. She moved toward the truck.

"Where's everyone else?" he asked.

She didn't seem to hear him, so he pulled the buds out of her ears.

"I'm trying to listen to a song," she said, shooting him a dirty look.

"How about listening to me instead. Where are the other kids?" he repeated.

"Already gone."

"What about Emily?"

"She's inside, I guess."

"I need her to let me into quarantine to check on that new dog," he said. "You want to come with?"

"I already saw her. She's skinny and gross looking." Taylor bit her lip. "How long before her fur grows back?"

"First we have to get rid of the mange. Once she's

healthy, she should have all her hair back in about two months. By then, she'll have put on a lot of weight, too."

"Emily can't keep her that long. She might need the space for another dog."

"Then let's hope she finds a good home for this one and the others."

Taylor nodded. "I'll wait in the truck."

"If that's what you want. There's a granola bar and a can of the pop you like on the passenger seat for you."

A look of pure scorn darkened her face. "I'm not a little kid, Seth."

No, but sometimes she sure acted like one. "You're welcome," he said. "Everybody gets hungry after school."

She didn't reply. The earbuds were back in place, and she was texting away.

"Be right back," he said, not expecting a reply.

A heavyset, gray-haired man who looked to be in his seventies sat at Mrs. Oakes's desk. Seth nodded. "I'm Seth Pettit, the shelter's vet this semester."

The older man's face lit up. "Nice to meet you. I'm Edgar Bell. I volunteer here on Mondays." They shook hands. "Too bad you're here for such a short time—we could use a long-term vet. We appreciate your service, though."

"Thanks. Is Emily around?"

"Check her office."

Although her door was open, Seth knocked before entering.

Emily was sorting through papers, and looked pleasantly surprised to see him. "Hi," she said.

Every time he saw that smile, he liked it more. She sure was pretty, especially in the silky blouse that fluttered when she moved. "I like that blue top."

The flush he'd come to anticipate colored her cheeks. "I dressed up a little today for orientation. Where's Taylor?"

"Waiting in the pickup. How'd she do this afternoon?"

"Pretty well. This year, I have eight kids, five from Taylor's school. I asked them to pair up and choose which day of the week to come. Taylor picked Thursdays. She'll be working with Cat, a girl from Jupiter High."

Not one of the Trenton kids. That was disappointing—she could use a friend at her school. Still, she'd found someone to work with, which was good news. He grinned. "So she finally she made a friend."

"I wouldn't exactly call them friends just yet, but they definitely could be."

Seth hoped. "Since I'm here, I may as well check on the quarantined dog."

"Of course. Would you mind going alone? I need to return phone calls from a couple of prospective adopters. The door to the quarantine hut is unlocked."

Seth left. The female mutt appeared perkier than she had a few days earlier, and her eyes were brighter. "Lookin' good," Seth told her before he returned to the pickup.

When he climbed in, he noted that the snack he'd brought Taylor were gone and the can of soda was empty. He wisely refrained from mentioning it. "How was orientation?" he asked as the pickup rolled down the driveway.

"Fine." She gave him a pained look. "I know Emily needs a veterinarian to volunteer at The Wagging Tail, but why does it have to be you?"

"We've already discussed this," he said. "What's going on?"

"Everyone knows that I live at your house."

Her unhappy expression made no secret of how she felt about that. "It's your house, too," he reminded her.

No comment. Seth shook his head. "If my volunteering here bothers you that much, I could tell Emily I changed my mind and quit," he said. "But I'd rather not leave her in the lurch."

Taylor mumbled something that sounded like, "You'll

probably just leave, anyway," but Seth wasn't sure. He wondered what that was about.

She made a face. "Just don't show up when I'm there."

JUST BEFORE ELEVEN O'CLOCK that night, Emily called Seth.

"Hello?" He sounded groggy.

She hated that she'd awakened him, hated bothering him in the evening, period. "It's Emily," she said, stepping outside to escape the awful barking in the kennel. "There's a German shepherd mix who's been here for almost a week, and I think he just had a seizure." She shivered in the brisk night air. "Now he's acting weird, and the other dogs are freaking out. Dr. Addison, the veterinarian before you, didn't uncover anything wrong with him, but obviously, something is very wrong."

She hoped that whatever it was could be fixed. Otherwise, no one would ever want to adopt him. "I need to get him out of the kennel and take him to the animal hospital, where they have a twenty-four-hour emergency clinic, only I…" Admitting this next part was unnerving. "I'm a little scared of him. I don't think I can get him into the car without help."

There were other volunteers she could call, but she wanted Seth's calm manner to soothe both the dog and herself. Because right now, she was a nervous wreck.

"From your place, that's a twenty-minute–plus drive," Seth said. "Let me scribble a note for Taylor and throw on some clothes, and I'll be there."

Thank goodness. Emily let out the breath she hadn't realized she'd been holding. "I'll be in the kennel," she said.

As wide-awake as she was, and right now she was crazy and wide-eyed, she was also weary. Having put in a long day that continued for hours after orientation, and had included setting up appointments with prospective dog adopters as well as several hours of work on the websites she maintained, she longed to climb into bed and sleep. Tonight that didn't seem likely.

But she was used to that. Over the last four years, she often spent a night or two a month dealing with some animal crisis or another.

Now that Seth was coming over, she thought about dashing upstairs to her apartment, trading the ratty sweats she'd changed into hours ago for jeans and a top, and pulling a comb through her hair. But she refused to leave the German shepherd for that long.

Seth would just have to take her as she was, sweats and all.

After what seemed like forever, but was actually no more than ten minutes, he was knocking at the door of the kennel.

At last. Emily let him in.

Chapter Five

Seth looked sleepy and needed a shave. But he was there. Emily wanted to hug him. Instead, she nodded toward the German shepherd's cage. "As you can hear, he's growling and barking and has all the other dogs upset," she said over the loud noise. "He's been at it nonstop. Plus he keeps bumping into the bars of his cage. I think he's gone crazy."

"Dogs often go temporarily blind after a seizure," Seth said, rolling up his sleeves. "Some bark and growl, too. Let me take a look at him. Then we'll get him out of the kennel, so that the other dogs will calm down. I'll need a muzzle."

He donned a pair of protective gloves and hunkered down in front of the cage, his broad shoulders straining his flannel shirt. Loose jeans outlined his muscular thighs.

Everything about him was big, including his hands, and yet Emily knew he performed surgery. Strong, yet precise, firm, yet tender... There was no telling what those capable hands would feel like on her bare skin. A shiver passed through her.

She gave herself a mental eye roll and bawled herself out. Now? She was lusting over Seth when the German shepherd was suffering from who knew what? The animals depended on her to keep them healthy and safe, and find them new homes. They came first. Always.

What was the matter with her? She'd certainly never lusted over Dr. Addison. But then, he was short and round and in his seventies.

Seth Pettit was a gorgeous man. He'd also given up his

night's rest to help this dog. She'd best get her mind on the matters at hand.

Careful to stay out of his way, she stood ready in case he needed her. Speaking in a low voice, he opened the door of the cage, slipped on the muzzle and gently guided the dog out. Although the barking increased to earsplitting levels, Seth continued to speak in the same low, calm voice.

Moments later, he straightened. "Let's figure out where to put him."

"Are we taking him to the hospital?" she asked.

"Not tonight. Right now he needs to be in a safe place. If I'm right, and the blindness and barking are after-effects of the seizure, eventually they'll fade away. In the morning, you'll want to take him to any local vet who sees dogs, and get tests to determine what caused the seizure."

Emily nodded. "One of the quarantine huts is empty."

"This could take hours," Seth said. "I'd rather put him someplace where you can be comfortable and accessible if he needs you."

Emily had to think about that. "I don't want him upsetting Susannah, so he can't stay in my apartment. But I could put him in the front office and sleep on the couch."

"That doesn't seem like a very comfortable place for you to bunk."

"I'll manage."

"All right. Let's go."

Seth hefted the animal, grunting with the effort.

As soon as they stepped into the darkness and closed the door to the kennel, the noise level inside dropped considerably.

"The other dogs are calmer already," Emily said.

Busy with his heavy load, Seth nodded, but didn't speak.

As they approached the office, the motion-detector lights flashed on. It was almost cold enough for Emily to see her breath.

She'd left a light on in the office. After quickly opening

the door, she stood back while Seth brought the dog inside and gently deposited him on the rug.

"If you'll wait here with him, I'll go back to the kennel and get his bed, so he'll have a familiar place to sleep," she said.

"I'll get it." Seth left.

The dog was still barking and growling. "If you stop making those noises, I'll remove that muzzle," Emily promised, to no avail.

She was relieved when Seth returned with the bedding. "Where do you want this?" he asked over the noise.

"How about right here, next to the couch."

He set up the animal's bed.

"Um, should we leave the muzzle on?" she asked. "So he doesn't bite?"

"Until he stops barking. What are you going to use for a pillow and blanket?"

"My apartment is upstairs," Emily explained. "I'll grab what I need from there."

"You live up there? Will Susannah be okay if you're down here?"

"She'll have to be."

"Want a hand with your stuff?" he asked.

For some reason, the thought of Seth alone upstairs with her at almost midnight was unnerving. "Why don't you stay with the dog, instead," she suggested.

She took a pillow and blanket downstairs, then went up again to say good-night to Susannah. The whippet was upset, probably because she could hear the German shepherd. Emily returned to the office, ready to say good-night to Seth.

"I should be okay now," she said over the barking. "Thanks for coming over tonight."

"I'll keep you company until he quiets down." Seth spoke equally loud.

"But you have to get up in a few hours."

"And you don't?"

Emily bit her lip. "I'll never be able to pay you back."

"You already are, by being nice to Taylor and building me a website."

"Taylor's not so bad." She hadn't started on his website yet. "I'm a little behind on things, but I'll be able to work on your site in a week or so. In the meantime, I'll email you a questionnaire. Fill it in and send it back, and we'll go from there."

Seth nodded. "I'll watch for it."

Her throat a little sore from keeping her voice raised, Emily set the pillows and blanket on the desk and sat on the couch.

She'd turned off all the office lights, and the only illumination came from the hallway, making the space feel cozy despite the shepherd's continuous barking. Seth joined her on the couch.

"You sure you want to bunk in here?" Seth asked. "You could probably sleep upstairs—as long as you're close enough to reach him if he needs you."

Emily shook her head. "I don't want to leave him alone. If my being here helps him in any way, I'm happy to do it."

"That's above and beyond."

She saw respect and admiration in his eyes, and it made her feel good. "It's all part of my job," she said.

THE GERMAN SHEPHERD was still going at it, but with less volume. Seth figured he'd quiet down soon. Then he would go home and get some sleep.

"Why did you decide to be a vet, Seth?" Emily asked beside him, her voice a welcome contrast to the dog's harsh barks.

Talking would help keep him alert, and he grabbed on to the question. "I like animals. They don't put on airs— they are who they are."

"They also love us unconditionally." The corners of her mouth lifted, as if the thought made her happy.

There was that, too.

"You mentioned family here," she said. "Taylor says your brother is a rancher."

"That's right, and my sister owns a restaurant. They're both married."

"Two siblings." Emily sighed. "You're so lucky. I don't have brothers or sisters."

"I'm not as lucky as you'd think."

"Oh?"

Not about to tell her that he'd pretty much ruined both relationships, he said, "Let's just say it's been a rocky road with those two, with most of the bumps caused by me." A road he was determined to smooth over. "What about your family?"

"Well, right now my mom and her husband, Bill, are on a six-week tour of Spain, Portugal and France. And by the way, Bill sold you your insurance policy."

"Bill Habegger is married to your mom? No kidding. Sometimes this town feels a lot smaller than it is." Seth was amazed. "I saw the photo on your desk and *knew* I recognized the man in it. Bill doesn't have that beard anymore."

"He shaved it right after that picture was taken."

"He mentioned that trip. He's a nice guy."

"He's great. Anyway, he and Mom live across town, not far from Prosperity Falls. Why did you leave Prosperity?"

"Both my parents died. I was eleven, and my older brother, Sly, and I went to live with an uncle we'd never met, in Iowa. He didn't want any girls, so Dani, that's my kid sister, stayed here and went into foster care."

Why was he telling Emily his story? She was probably bored. Only with her lower lip caught between her teeth, and her eyes wide, she didn't look bored.

"I'm sorry, Seth. That can't have been easy."

She had no idea. "No, but it helps me understand what

Taylor's going through. Anyway, Dani got the best end of the deal. Her foster mother adopted her." Seth and Sly hadn't fared as well.

"The uncle who took you in didn't adopt you?"

"He didn't exactly like kids," Seth said. "Another thing about Dani—she married her best friend. Nick." Seth had met Nick when he and Sly had returned to Prosperity, before Seth had left for what he'd thought was for good. He'd never imagined that Dani would fall in love with the guy. Some people were lucky that way.

"What about you? Have you lived here all your life?" he asked.

"My mom and I have, but not my father. He left when I was in grade school."

Seth shook his head. "You, Taylor and me—we've all been through rough times."

"You and I survived to tell the tale, and Taylor will, too. Have you ever been married?"

"No, but I came close once. You?" he asked.

"I was engaged once."

"Really." Seth was surprised. Not that she'd been engaged, but that whoever she'd been with had somehow lost her. "What happened?"

"Are you sure you want to hear the story?"

"Why not?" He nodded at the dog, which was still barking. "We have time."

"I'll give you the five-minute version. I met Harvey when I interviewed him about adopting one of the dogs."

"Interviewed?" Seth asked.

She nodded. "The animals at the shelter have been abandoned and some have been abused. They need plenty of TLC, and I'm not about to let just anyone walk out of here with one of them."

"That makes sense. About your ex…"

"He's an architect. After he adopted a dog, he offered to help me turn the garage here into the kennel area. Later he built the two quarantine huts. Somewhere during those two projects, we started dating. Fast-forward almost a year. We got engaged and rented an apartment together. Six months later, he got a job offer from a company on the East Coast."

"And you didn't want to leave Prosperity," Seth guessed.

"No, I was willing to go with him. I figured I could find someone to run The Wagging Tail and that I'd start a shelter in our new city." She splayed her fingers and glanced at her hands. "But Harvey didn't want me there. That's when I moved in upstairs."

Seth couldn't believe it. "Harvey was a damn fool."

"Thanks," she said. "I agree, but it took me a while to realize it."

"Did you love him?" he asked. Not that it was any of his business.

"I wish I could say no, but I did. I thought he loved me, too." She sighed. "I was wrong."

Seth wanted to deck the bastard for hurting her. Hardly aware of his actions, he put his arm around her and pulled her close to his side.

"It's been almost a year and a half since he left, and I'm over him now," she said.

"I loved Taylor's mom, too," he admitted. "I just didn't realize it until she and Taylor split."

"Have you been in a relationship since?"

"A couple, but nothing long-lasting." He seemed doomed that way. "What about you?"

Emily shook her head. "I've been too busy with the shelter and my web business."

They were both quiet then. The barking continued, but at a slower pace. Seth yawned and stretched, and so did Emily.

"In the spring, my landlord is putting the house where Taylor and I live on the market," he said. "It has good bones, and with upgrades and a couple coats of paint, I think I can make it into a real nice place."

"You're going to buy it?"

"If I can save up the money for the down payment."

Emily bit her lip. "I wish I could pay you something."

"I didn't tell you to make you feel bad. I just thought you should know." He couldn't have said why.

She nodded. After a long pause, she asked, "Do you have any nieces or nephews?"

"Two nieces, both my brother's."

"That's great. I hope to have kids someday."

"You should," he said. "You'll make a great mom."

She angled her head. "What makes you say that?"

"The way you mother the dogs here."

"Aww, that's so sweet." A smile lit her face. "Thanks for staying with me. You're a pretty cool guy, Dr. Seth Pettit."

"Ditto. Hear that?" He cupped his hand to his ear.

"Hear what?" Emily asked.

"Exactly. The dog finally stopped barking." Seth stood and went to his patient.

The shepherd was sitting on his haunches near the desk. Speaking in a low voice so as not to startle him, Seth approached and shone a penlight into his eyes. A moment later, he switched it off and shook his head. "He's still blind, but I think it's safe to remove his muzzle. You might want to get out of here until I gauge whether he's going to bite."

Emily shook her head and joined him. "I'm not afraid of him anymore."

The dog seemed relieved to be rid of the muzzle. Seth didn't blame him. He could probably leave now, but was oddly reluctant to go.

For the first time since he'd arrived, he finally looked Emily over. She was wearing baggy sweats, with her hair pulled into a loose ponytail. She glanced down at herself and laughed. "You're one lucky man, Seth. I don't think any other guy has ever seen me looking like this."

Seth had never met a woman like her, able to laugh at herself at her own expense. His mouth quirked. "The joys of animal care. You look cute."

"No, I don't."

"To me, you do."

Her laughter died but not her smile. In the dim light, her eyes seemed to sparkle. He couldn't look away.

Then a yawn escaped. Emily followed suit, then nudged him with her elbow. "Go home, Seth, and get some sleep."

It was time. At the door, it seemed natural to kiss her. He leaned in, cupped her face in his hands and slid his lips lightly across hers. Just a little taste. A casual good-night.

It wasn't enough for him. By the yearning expression on her face, not her, either.

Her arms stole around his neck and her soft lips opened, inviting him to explore. The long, deep kiss heated his blood and hardened his body.

He wanted more. A lot more.

But this wasn't the time or the place—or the woman. If and when he found the time, she would be someone who wanted what he did—release without complications. It was obvious to him that Emily wasn't like that. No doubt she'd expect loving words and feelings, when experience had proved time and again that Seth was lousy at both. As badly as he wanted to get nice and intimate with her, that path would lead straight to trouble. And he already had enough of that in his life.

Reluctantly, he pulled back.

Emily's eyes fluttered open. She looked thoroughly kissed, slightly dazed and extremely sexy.

To hell with smart. He knew he'd be back for more.

He cleared his throat and forced himself to open the door. "Good night, Emily."

"Good night, Seth."

As he walked out, the sound of his name on her lips lingered sweetly with him.

Chapter Six

On Thursday afternoon Emily was in the front office, filling Mrs. Oakes in on Taylor and Cat, when Taylor traipsed in, hauling a bulging backpack that had to weigh a ton.

It was a cold, cloudy day and the wind buffeted the old windows. For the first time this year, Emily had cranked up the baseboard heaters, and both she and Mrs. Oakes wore thick cardigans.

Apparently Taylor hadn't gotten the message that summer was over. She wore a zip-up, short-sleeved, cotton hoodie. The mere sight of those bare arms gave Emily goose bumps.

She greeted the girl with a smile. "Welcome back, Taylor. It's good to see you. Aren't you cold?"

"A little, but I'm okay."

Emily introduced her to Mrs. Oakes and said, "As soon as Cat arrives, I'll put you both to work."

Taylor bit her lip. "Do you think she'll come?"

"I haven't heard otherwise," Emily replied.

Moments later, she arrived. Cat, too, had dressed for warm weather, in a tank top that barely covered her stomach, and a lightweight shrug. Mentally shaking her head at both girls, Emily greeted her and, again introduced Mrs. Oakes.

The two girls exchanged perfunctory smiles and studied each other warily. Determined to put them at ease, Emily brought them into her office and directed them to sit down in front of her desk.

"A new dog came in yesterday," she said. "She's in quarantine right now and awaiting the results of her lab tests."

Seth had stopped by late yesterday afternoon to examine and vaccinate the animal. Still reeling from their kisses and not ready to face him, Emily had made sure she was out, interviewing a prospective adopter.

This morning, she'd finally pulled herself together. She needed Seth for his veterinary skills, but she wasn't ready for anything else. Even if she had enjoyed his company the other night. Make that *thoroughly* enjoyed.

Since meeting Seth—since those steamy good-night kisses—her body had awakened from a long sleep. Her mind might tell her she wasn't ready for intimacy, but the rest of her wanted it.

Not that anything was going to happen. She couldn't risk jeopardizing the professional relationship she had with Seth. He seemed to enjoy working with the dogs, and she couldn't help but cross her fingers that he just might decide to stay on after Taylor's semester of community service ended. Okay, maybe Emily also wanted to protect herself from becoming involved with him and then getting hurt. And right now, she wasn't going to think about Seth Pettit and his kisses.

"Let's go over what I want you to do while you're here," she said. "We walk our dogs at least once a day, and I'd like you to do that. You'll start with one dog each, and when you bring them back, you'll walk another."

"Are we supposed to go together?" Cat asked, glancing at Taylor.

Emily nodded. "We keep the leashes in the kennel room."

"How is the dog who had the seizure?" Taylor asked. "Is he okay?"

Emily figured she knew about that. "Seth told you about him?" she asked.

The girl nodded.

Emily bet he hadn't mentioned the good-night kisses. Oh, could he kiss… *Hey,* she reminded herself, *I'm not going to think about him or that anymore.* She wasn't.

Cat was giving her a blank look. "You have no idea what we're talking about," Emily said. "Why don't you explain, Taylor?"

The teen jumped in eagerly. "Remember the German shepherd in the kennel? We saw him during orientation? He had a seizure."

Cat looked stricken. "What's wrong with him?"

"Seth diagnosed him with epilepsy," Emily said. "That was confirmed later, when I took him to the animal hospital for tests."

"I told you he knew about dogs." Taylor almost sounded proud of her guardian.

Cat gave a sage nod. "A boy in my class has epilepsy. Once, he had a seizure in the lunchroom. It was scary. After, they took him to the nurse's office. Now he takes something to control the seizures."

"Seth said the German shepherd was blind and barking like crazy," Taylor said.

Emily bit her lip. "I was worried, and awfully relieved when Seth came. He said that blindness and constant barking sometimes follow a seizure, and that eventually they fade. He was right about that, too—a few hours after the seizure, the shepherd was back to his normal self."

Not so with Emily. She'd been keyed up for hours, and not just because of the animal's unnerving epsiode. Seth's potent kisses had been pretty stimulating.

"Since we're talking about the German shepherd, why don't you walk him and the little short-haired mix first?" she said. "Those two get along pretty well."

"I don't know…" Taylor gnawed on her baby fingernail. "What if he has another seizure?"

"Just like that boy in Cat's class, he's taking medicine

now to prevent that," Emily assured her. "He should be okay."

"But what if he isn't?"

"Then contact me immediately on my cell or my pager."

"Where do you want us to take them?" Cat asked.

"This is a rural area, so anyplace around the shelter is good. A fifteen to twenty minute walk is ideal. They're going to want to run free, but please don't let them off their leashes. We don't want them to turn back into strays. It's chilly this afternoon. Would either of you like a sweater or jacket? I have extras."

Both girls accepted the offer. Five minutes later, they leashed the two dogs and left.

Mrs. Oakes shook her head. "What is it with teenagers and skimpy clothes?"

"I have no idea," Emily said. "At least they were smart enough to borrow sweaters. Cat and Taylor will be working together the whole semester. Do you think they'll make friends?"

"Of course. If walking those dogs together doesn't do it, I don't know what will."

TAYLOR AND CAT headed down a path that crossed a wide field. Taylor was in charge of the German shepherd. Emily was right—he was eager to run. Straining at his leash, he pulled her along at a rapid clip. "He wants off his leash," she said.

"So does my dog," Cat replied. "You heard Emily—we can't."

"I'm having trouble keeping up. Slow down," Taylor ordered, but the shepherd didn't listen. She was almost running now, and starting to sweat despite the cold. She wanted to pull off the sweater she'd borrowed from Emily, but didn't dare let go of the leash.

Finally, tired of racing along, she dug in her heels. "Stop!"

To her surprise, the command worked. The German shepherd obeyed, coming to an abrupt stop.

Cat tried the same thing with her dog, with the same result. They went on at a slower pace.

"What's your favorite class?" Cat asked, still huffing a little.

Taylor felt more comfortable around her now. "At my other school, it was band. I don't like any of the classes at Trenton." The only reason she was doing community service was because if she didn't, she'd get in a lot of trouble.

"Trenton has a band," Cat said. "I heard them when our school played yours in basketball last year."

"Yeah, but I don't want to join," Taylor said.

She wasn't planning to stay in Prosperity that long, and was doing everything she could think of to go home to San Diego. All she needed was a place to stay.

Seth wouldn't mind if she left. He'd be happy. He didn't want her around—he'd proved that before, when he'd walked away from her and her mom. He was taking care of her now only because he had to.

"What's your instrument?" Cat asked.

"I don't have one anymore, but I used to play the trumpet. Do you play anything?"

"I took piano for a few years, but I'm into art now. I'm going to be an artist someday."

Taylor thought that was cool. She gestured at Cat's boots, an awesome lime green, with blue stars on the toes. "Did you paint those yourself?"

Cat nodded.

"They're super cute. I don't know what I'm going to be."

"Maybe a musician."

Taylor wasn't into playing music now. "I don't think so."

"If you could do anything you wanted in the whole world, what would you pick?" Cat asked. She had this funny way of angling her head when she asked a question.

Taylor knew what she *didn't* want to be—a secretary.

Her mom had been one, and had hated it. Taylor had no idea what she wanted to do when she was out on her own, but she definitely wanted enough money to go on vacations and buy clothes anytime she wanted, and not have to worry about paying bills. "I haven't decided yet," she said. "We should turn around now."

"I love dogs," Cat said as they steered the animals toward the shelter.

"Me, too. If I didn't, I wouldn't be doing my community service here."

Cat looked wistful. "I wish I could have one, but my mom is allergic. We have a tropical fish tank instead." She made a face. "I like fish, but they can't take a walk with you or cuddle up. What do you think of Emily?"

"She's okay." Taylor wasn't happy that Seth was volunteering at the shelter, but it wasn't Emily's fault that she'd needed a vet exactly when she'd met him. Anyway, for all his faults, he definitely knew animals.

Cat's head angled sideways. "How come you call your dad Seth?"

Since Taylor had moved to Prosperity, no one had asked. She didn't mind explaining. "He's not my dad," she said. "He's my guardian."

"Why aren't you living with your parents?"

Taylor was aware that Seth had explained the situation to the teachers and his family, but none of the kids in her school knew.

"Because I don't have a dad, and my mom died in a car accident," she explained, with barely a quaver in her voice.

Cat's eyes widened. "Bummer."

"Yeah."

It wasn't just the secretary job that her mom had disliked. She hadn't liked Taylor much, either. Lately they'd been fighting a lot, their last battle at breakfast on the very day of the accident.

Taylor felt sick when she thought about the way she'd

acted and the things she'd said that morning. Her parting words to her mom had been mean and hateful. She pushed the painful memory from her mind and concentrated on the dog, which was sniffing something on the ground in front of them.

"Did your dad pass away, too?" Cat asked.

"I don't know." Taylor shrugged. "I never met him. My Mom wasn't sure who he was."

"Oh. I know the names of my birth mom and dad, and that they were sixteen when she got pregnant with me. They gave me up for adoption."

"Wow," Taylor said. She couldn't imagine how that must feel. "Do you ever see them?"

"Nope. I don't even want to. Is Seth a longtime family friend or something?"

Taylor shook her head. She hated talking about this, but Cat had asked. "When I was little, he lived with my mom and me. Then one day, he just picked up and left. My mom was so upset that she moved us to another town."

"That sucks."

It had. Taylor was never, ever going to trust Seth again.

"Then how come you live with him now?"

"Because my mom had something in her will about him being my guardian." Wanting to change the subject, she said, "We're almost back."

"I'm ready for a break. Unless Emily wants us to walk the other two dogs right away."

Taylor sighed. "She probably does."

Over a sandwich on Thursday, Seth studied his sorry bank account statement and stressed about the week's less-than-full schedule of appointments. At this rate, he'd never pull together the money he needed to buy the house. And he wanted that almost as badly as he wanted his relationship with Taylor to improve.

Things had to change, and fast. He needed to sharpen

his focus on building the business, and not let other stuff distract him. Namely Emily and The Wagging Tail. He wasn't sorry he'd kissed her the other night, but it shouldn't have happened. Because since then, he spent way too much time thinking about her and wanting more.

As for the shelter, he wished he hadn't agreed to volunteer there. Sure, caring for those poor animals felt good. But so far, the little amount of time he was supposed to spend with them each week had turned into a bigger commitment than he'd expected.

Briefly he considered quitting. But no, he wasn't about to go back on his promise. Want to or not, he would stick it out until Taylor finished her community service at the end of the semester. On the positive side, Emily had agreed to get his website up and running, and that would probably help his business. Which reminded him that he needed to fill in the questionnaire she'd sent, and return it to her ASAP.

Suddenly his cell phone rang, the screen indicating a call from his brother. Pleasantly surprised, Seth picked up. "Hey, Sly."

"Got a laboring heifer in trouble," Sly said by way of a hello.

"What's the problem?"

"She's been laboring for hours now, but the calf isn't coming. I tried to grab hold of it and so did Ace." Sly's foreman. "No luck. We need your help."

Words Seth had never thought to hear from his brother. "I'll be right there," he said, already on his way to the pickup.

Fifteen minutes later he pulled up the long driveway of Pettit Ranch. His brother had done well for himself. Everything about the ranch sang of his prosperity—freshly painted buildings, hills dotted with livestock, men hard at work, and a house anyone would be proud to live in.

In the not too distant future, Seth's house—it *would* be his—would look just as fine.

Sly was waiting for him near the barn.

"Hey," Seth said.

His brother nodded and tipped the brim of his hat. He stood a hair over six feet tall, a half-inch shorter than Seth, with the same silvery-blue eyes. Dani had the Pettit eyes, too.

Sly's hands were low on his hips and he wore a guarded look, as if he expected trouble from Seth. This was a good opportunity to prove that any trouble between them was long past.

"The heifer's in the calving pen," Sly said. "This way."

He led Seth around the barn and past two outbuildings. The cow was inside a room set aside for problem births, lying on her side. Her breathing was labored, and she made pained noises. Ace stood nearby, watching closely.

"Have you tried chains or a calf puller?" Seth asked.

"Twice in the last hour," his brother replied.

Seth examined the bovine and made a quick decision. "She's carrying twins. She needs a Cesarean—now. I could use your help—both of you."

They nodded. After rolling up his sleeves and donning his lab coat, Seth shaved the area where he would make the incision. He administered the anesthetic, and while waiting for it to work, disinfected the cow's side. When he was sure she was numb, he got busy.

He didn't speak again until he'd opened her up. "Look at that—one of the calves is blocking the birth canal. No wonder she couldn't deliver."

He pulled out the calves, putting one in Sly's care and the other in Ace's. While they saw to the newborns, Seth cleaned the dam's—the mother's—abdominal cavity. Then he sutured her up. He didn't draw an easy breath until he'd tied off the threads.

"As soon as she recovers from the anesthetic, put her in

with her calves," he said. "Meanwhile, I suggest you tube feed them at least once, to make sure they get the nourishment they need to grow stronger."

"You set it up," Sly said. "Ace and I will make sure it happens."

Seth put the tubes in place and stuck around through the first feeding. "Those calves look better already," he noted. "Dams don't always know how to take care of two at the same time, so keep an eye on them."

"I'll stay with them tonight," Ace volunteered. He was a good man who knew his cattle.

Seth shook hands with him, and left him with the animals. Then it was just him and Sly, heading out of the building.

"Thanks, brother," Sly said.

Seth nodded and removed his lab coat, folding it with the soiled area inside. "Where do I wash up?"

"In the barn.

When Seth finished, he dried his hands and rolled down his sleeves.

For a few moments he and Sly stood facing each other. Now that the excitement was over, familiar uneasiness filled the air. Seth shifted his weight and picked up his medical bag. "All right then," he said.

He was turning to leave when Sly spoke. "If I don't offer you a cup of coffee, Lana will have a fit."

The man had a good five inches and seventy pounds on his wife, but she had him wrapped around her baby finger.

Seth checked his watch. "I've got a little while before I pick up Taylor, and I could use some coffee. Is Lana still at work?"

She owned two successful day-care facilities, and took her kids, ages four and eighteen months, to work with her.

Sly nodded. "She should be home around four. Johanna and Mark will be surprised to see twin calves."

Seth thought it was sweet that they'd named their son and daughter after his and Sly's parents.

He liked his brother's big, cozy kitchen, which was warm and colorful. There was evidence of his children everywhere, from the bright finger-paintings attached to the fridge with magnets, to the overflowing box of toys in the corner.

Sly had the family that he, Seth and Dani had all wanted, and Seth envied him. But he wasn't the kind of man to keep a relationship going for long—he didn't know how.

Sly pulled out a container of oatmeal raisin cookies his part-time housekeeper had made, and Seth helped himself. "These are great," he said, chewing with relish.

"I'll let Mrs. Rutland know you like them."

They nursed their coffees in silence. In the mounting tension, Seth began to wish he'd turned down his brother's invitation.

After a while, Sly cleared his throat. "How does Taylor like Trenton High?"

"According to her, everything about it sucks. She hates me, too." Seth wondered how she was doing on her first working afternoon at The Wagging Tail. He hoped she liked the work enough to stick around the whole semester and get her community service credit.

The corners of his brother's mouth lifted in a semblance of a smile. "Sounds just like someone I used to know."

"Come on," Seth said. "I was never as bad as Taylor."

Sly sat back and eyed him. "Does she get into fistfights with other kids?"

"Not that I know of."

"Has she ever tossed a brick through a store window and been picked up by the police?"

Seth shook his head and let out a self-deprecating laugh. "I was a little butthead, wasn't I?"

"And then some."

"You were no picnic, either, Sly."

"Hey, I did the best I could."

It was the closest either of them had come to apologizing for the past. They hadn't had an easy time, with their uncle randomly screaming at them for some offense, and occasionally using his fists or his belt to make a point. When he wasn't ignoring them and letting them fend for themselves.

Seth and his brother left a lot unsaid, things that needed airing. But the moment passed.

No surprise there. They'd never been forthcoming with their feelings. Not to each other.

Seth checked his watch. "It's getting late, and we both have things to do."

"Right." Sly stood and, without fanfare, ushered him to the door. "Thanks for your help today. How much do I owe you, and where do I send the check?"

As badly as Seth needed the money, he wasn't about to take a penny from his brother. "I'm not going to charge my own brother."

"Free appointments don't pay the bills."

That was Sly, the practical one. Since Seth had left Prosperity at the age of seventeen, he'd learned to be practical, too. Otherwise he would never have earned his GED or attended college and vet school.

"I'm doing okay," he lied. Soon enough, he would be— God willing. "If you want to pay me, tell your rancher friends about me. Word of mouth is the best way to build my practice."

He and his brother shook hands. Sly didn't invite him to come back, but at least he'd sought him out for his veterinary skills. That counted for something.

As Seth headed for the pickup, a call came in from a rancher whose cow had gone lame.

When he disconnected, he was frowning. He needed to check on the animal, but that would make him late to pick up Taylor. She'd have to wait around at the shelter. He didn't envy Emily that.

Chapter Seven

Taylor didn't look happy as she disconnected from her cell phone. "Seth is going to be late."

Cat had already been gone a good half hour and Mrs. Oakes had just left. It was getting dark, and Emily guessed that the girl wanted to go home. "I need to go out and run a few errands. I'm happy to drop you off on the way," she offered.

The teen brightened. "You'd do that?"

Emily nodded. "You'd better call Seth back and make sure it's okay."

Five minutes later, the girl was seated in the passenger seat of Emily's hatchback. Furious rain pelted the car. "It's really coming down," Emily said.

"It doesn't rain like this in San Diego."

"Montana is a lot different than where you're from. Soon it's going to be much colder here."

"Then it'll snow." Taylor actually looked excited. "I've never seen snow, except in pictures or on TV."

Emily laughed. "Trust me, you're going to see tons of the stuff."

Wondering how Taylor and Cat had gotten along, but not wanting to ask point-blank, she skirted the subject. "How did you like your first day of community service?"

"I wasn't sure what to expect, but walking the dogs was kind of fun."

"Did Cat enjoy it, too?"

"I guess. I mean, she didn't say she hated it."

"Do you and she have anything in common?"

"We both like dogs."

That was a start. "Anything else?"

"I don't know," Taylor said. "Cat is an artist. I'm not. She painted her boots."

"I wondered about that." The light ahead turned red, and Emily braked to a stop. "What about you, Taylor. What do you like to do?"

"Nothing much," she said with a shrug.

"What do you do when you're not in school and not studying?"

Taylor fiddled with the zipper of her hoodie. "I talk on FaceTime with my friends in San Diego."

"I'll bet you miss them."

"A lot."

"Do you think you'll see them again?"

"Definitely."

"When is Seth taking you back for a visit?"

"I don't know." She compressed her lips. "It doesn't really matter, because I'm going to live there again."

"You mean when you graduate from high school."

"Way before then."

Did Seth know about this? With Taylor so unhappy, he probably did. Adjusting to their situation couldn't be easy for either of them, and Emily's heart went out to them both. If only she could do something to help. "But Seth plans to buy the house he's renting, for you two to live in permanently," she said.

Taylor didn't respond, just stared out the passenger window so that Emily couldn't see her face. Who knew what she was thinking?

The rain had slowed enough that Emily was able to relax and take in the surroundings. In the growing darkness, she noted that they were in a modest area of neatly maintained yards and houses. "This is a nice neighborhood," she said.

"I guess. The next street is ours."

Emily turned onto a narrow street of one- and two-story

homes. Cheery light shone through the windows. Families were inside, catching up on each others' days and cooking dinner. Although it had been decades since Emily's father had walked out, suddenly her heart ached for what she'd never had. A house and two loving parents.

"It's the one with the dark green trim," Taylor said, pointing ahead.

Emily pulled into the driveway and studied the nondescript two-story. It wasn't the Ritz, but it looked good to her. Taylor didn't know how lucky she was. "This is nice," she said.

Another shrug conveyed that she wasn't impressed.

"I always dreamed of living in a place like this," Emily admitted.

"Why didn't you?"

"Because my parents split up and my mom could only afford a one-bedroom apartment."

"My mom and I lived in apartments, too. Our last complex had a pool. Sometimes my friends came over to swim."

"That sounds fun."

"I liked it." Taylor lifted her hips and extracted a house key from her jeans pocket. "Thanks for the ride."

"You're welcome. I'll see you next Thursday. Don't forget to ask Seth about the fund-raising party. I really need you there."

"I'll ask him tonight."

Emily waited in the driveway until the girl dashed up the walk, unlocked the door and disappeared inside. Just as she started to back out, Seth drove up. Her heart actually lifted in her chest, as if she was a teenage girl Taylor's age. She gave a mental eye roll. That had to stop.

SETH RECOGNIZED EMILY's light blue hatchback. He hadn't expected to see her, and wasn't sure he liked the hitch in his gut.

Wanting to thank her and find out how Taylor had behaved on her first day at The Wagging Tail, he pulled up next to her, set the brake and exited the pickup. By the time he walked to the driver's side of her car, she'd put her window down.

"Looks like you've been busy," she said.

Seth glanced down at himself. Not anticipating a second call this afternoon, he'd brought only one lab coat with him. It had been too filthy to use twice. Smears of mud and God knew what else stained the front of his shirt. "This can be a pretty gross job," he said, his mouth quirking.

"You know I understand." She smiled and it was like the sun came out.

He leaned down, resting his arms on the open window. "It's been quite a day," he said, wanting to tell her about it. "I did a C-section on one of the cows at my brother's ranch and delivered twin calves. Then I stopped at another ranch and took care of a lame cow with a nasty abscess. I washed the goo off my hands and arms, but didn't have a spare shirt with me. Thanks for giving Taylor a ride home."

"No problem. I needed to go out, anyway, and pick up dog food."

Seth nodded. Although Taylor was likely in her room, wearing her earbuds and bent over her cell phone, he lowered his voice. "How'd she do today?"

"Not bad. I think she enjoyed it."

"Did she and the girl she's doing community service with get along all right?"

"You mean Cat. As far as I could tell, they did fine together."

Seth was relieved. "She sure could use a friend in town."

"On the drive here, she mentioned moving back to San Diego before she graduates high school."

"Did she now?" Given how much she disliked Prosperity, Seth wasn't surprised. "That's not happening," he said. "This is her home now."

"You might want to make sure she understands that."

"Trust me, I tell her all the time. Not that she hears me."

"Maybe if you share your thoughts about fixing up the house after you buy it, or ask her for her input, she'll change her mind. When I was her age, I would've been thrilled to live in a house like this."

"You told her about that?" he asked, frowning.

"You haven't." She looked surprised. "Was it supposed to be a secret?"

"No, I just… I wasn't planning on telling her until I have the money for the down payment."

"In case your plans fall through, you don't want to disappoint her." Emily bit her lip. "Sorry I said anything."

"Don't worry about it. I'll get there. Hell, I probably *should* say something. Wouldn't make much difference, though—she isn't interested in hearing about any plans for a future with me in it." He was about at the end of his rope. "The girl could use some counseling."

"That sounds like a good idea. Have you talked with the school?"

He nodded. "They gave me a couple names, but Taylor won't have anything to do with therapists. She thinks she's fine."

"Gosh, that sounds challenging."

For some reason, knowing Emily sympathized helped. It was good to be able to talk to her about this. "Hardest thing I've ever had to deal with."

They shared a long look, and just like that, electricity charged the air between them. Seth wanted to kiss her as he had the other night, his desire so strong he barely restrained himself.

Even in the dark, he could see Emily's expressive eyes responding with the same heat. She *wanted* him to kiss her.

He almost groaned. With very little effort he could lean in a fraction and do just that.

But Taylor could look through the window at any time,

and his shirt was filthy. He straightened. "I'll let you go now."

"Right." Emily shook her head as if to clear it. "Before I leave, you should know that I invited the community-service kids to a pizza brainstorming party for my annual fund-raiser. It will be a week from tomorrow, after school, upstairs in my apartment. I'm not sure exactly what time we'll finish, but not too late."

Seth nodded. "Are parents and guardians invited?"

"The more, the merrier, so if you'd like to come…"

Oh, he wanted to be there, all right. Just him and Emily, with the curtains pulled. That wasn't going to happen, but a guy could fantasize.

"Taylor will be there—that is, if I can convince her to come," he said. "Of course, if I try to do that, she probably *won't* come."

They shared a smile at that.

"She acted as if she wanted to be there," Emily said. "She said she was going to ask you about it."

"That's a good sign. Before she met you, she didn't show interest in anything in Prosperity. All that mattered were her friends in San Diego. Now she's involved with the shelter and might even have a local friend." Seth shook his head in admiration. "You're a miracle worker." A beautiful one, to boot.

Emily laughed self-consciously. "Credit the shelter dogs for any changes you see in Taylor," she said. "Spending time with them… No matter what we do or how many mistakes we make, they love us. With all that trust and love, we can't help but be our best selves."

Seth couldn't have said it better himself, and agreed wholeheartedly. Emily amazed him with her insights.

The more he got to know her, the better he liked her.

"Taylor really likes dogs, Seth," she went on. "I know you want to wait until things settle down, but maybe you should get one now."

"I'll think about it."

Overhead, thunder boomed and a shard of lightning split the sky.

Emily glanced upward, into the blackness. "It's going to pour again." She nodded toward the pickup. "You'd better put your truck away and hurry inside."

"Right." Forgetting that he shouldn't touch her, Seth reached through the window and ran his finger across her cheek. Her responding shiver only ratcheted up his desire for her. He dropped his hand and stepped back. "I'll see you soon. Have a good weekend."

"You, too."

He climbed into the pickup and put up the window, just in time. Furious rain pelted the ground and pounded on the roof of the truck. Instead of pulling into the carport, he turned in his seat and watched Emily back down the driveway.

He didn't look away until her taillights disappeared down the street.

WHEN EMILY HEARD the sound of a honking horn Saturday night, she grabbed her jacket. "I'm going out with Monica and Bridget, and I'll be back in a few hours," she told Susannah. "Behave."

She headed outside, where her two best friends were waiting for her in Bridget's Mini Cooper. They hadn't seen each other in weeks, and on the twenty-minute drive across town, they caught up on each other's lives.

"Have you heard from your parents?" Monica asked as soon as Emily settled into the back seat.

"Since they landed in Madrid, I've had two emails from them," Emily said. "Now that they've recovered from a bad case of jet lag, they're having a great time."

"Bowling on a Saturday night isn't as cool as touring Europe, but this should be fun," Monica said. "If we're lucky, we just might meet some cute guys."

Petite, perfectly proportioned and outgoing, she had no trouble attracting men.

"You'll probably meet several," Bridget lamented in an envious tone. "You always do, and I hate you for it."

At five feet eight and a half, the strawberry blonde was bigger-boned than Emily, with a pretty face. Although she had a ready laugh and dropped wisecracks like a pro around Emily and Monica, she tended to be more reserved in mixed company, which made meeting men difficult.

"Just because I make friends easily with the opposite sex doesn't mean I've had any luck finding my Mr. Right," Monica lamented. At thirty, she'd already been married and divorced.

None of them had had very good luck with that.

After a glum silence, Bridget straightened her shoulders. "We're not here to moan and groan about our sorry love lives. Tonight is about having a great time. First on the agenda, bowling-alley dinner."

"I've been thinking about the hot dogs and greasy fries all day." Emily licked her lips.

"Don't forget root beer," Monica said. "The high-cal kind. Why not? We'll bowl off the excess calories."

They all laughed.

"So, Emily, how's the new volunteer veterinarian working out?" Monica asked.

Over the phone, Emily had mentioned Seth and Taylor, and how the teen had come to live with him. He kissed like a dream, but she wasn't going to mention that. It wouldn't happen again, so why get them all excited?

"Seth is really good at his job," she said. "I'm going to build a website for him." She would start that as soon as he returned the questionnaire she'd emailed.

Bridget glanced at her in the rearview mirror. "He's going to pay you?"

Emily shook her head. "This is my way of paying *him* for volunteering at the shelter."

"What about the poor, motherless teenage girl who lives with him?" Monica asked.

"Taylor. Community service only started this past week, and Thursday was her first real day to volunteer. She wasn't exactly Miss Happy Face, but she did okay. Let's hope things work out."

Monica caught them up on her job as an interior designer for commercial businesses, and Bridget shared a story about a customer at the consignment women's clothing store she owned. After that, they lapsed into a comfortable silence. It was a crisp fall night, with a full moon.

"A moon like that puts me in a romantic mood." Bridget sounded wistful. "Too bad there isn't anyone to get romantic with."

"You'll meet someone," Monica said. "And so will I. You, too, Emily." She snorted. "If you're ever ready."

"I will be, but not just yet."

"I wish you'd get over Harvey. He doesn't deserve for you to waste your time pining over him."

"As I keep reminding you, I *am* over him. You know how busy I am. Between the shelter and my web business, it's a wonder I ever get out and have fun."

"Don't use your passion for those dogs or your website business as excuses," Bridget warned. "Otherwise, you just might end up like my aunt Arlene."

The fifty-five-year-old woman, victim of a nasty divorce some fifteen years earlier, had never recovered, and was lonely and unhappy.

Emily wasn't about to let that happen. "I promise," she said. "If I'm still single five years from now, you both have my permission to smack me upside the head."

Bridget turned into the parking lot of the bowling alley. "Look at all these cars," she said. "It's busy tonight."

The bowling alley was crowded and noisy with families, couples and singles like them. There were no available lanes, so they left Emily's name with the woman in charge.

While they waited for a lane to open up, they rented shoes. Emily's were scuffed and ill-fitting, but that was part of the bowling experience. Next, they bought dinner, and sat down at a small table to eat.

"What'd I tell you—there are tons of cute guys here without dates," Monica commented as she licked ketchup from a fry.

"So I see." Bridget nodded at a male about their age who was headed for one of the bowling lanes. "Look at the man in the faded jeans and flannel shirt."

"I'm looking," Monica murmured. "What do you think, Em? Is he hot or what?"

He *was* good-looking, but he couldn't compare with a certain volunteer veterinarian. Emily pushed the thought away. "He's not bad."

"Not bad?" Monica gaped at her. "Maybe you need glasses."

No, she just needed to stop fantasizing about Seth Pettit.

"Emily, party of three, lane six is ready for you," a female voice announced over the PA.

After quickly disposing their trash, Emily and her friends headed there.

"You drove tonight, Bridget," Emily said when they'd settled their things on the bench seating. "You're up first."

Bridget's ball rimmed the gutter before glancing against two pins. She made a face. "Pathetic." As soon as the machine returned her ball, she bowled again. When only one pin toppled over, she shrugged good-naturedly. "At least I tried."

Monica went next. She did an odd little twist and released the ball, sending it speeding toward the pins. At the last second, it veered left and cut a neat swath through the left third of them.

"Darn!" She compressed her lips. The second roll toppled three more pins. "Six," she said. "Whoop tee doo."

"Way to swivel your hips, though," Emily said.

They were all laughing when Bridget glanced to the left. Sobering, she leaned in a little and lowered her voice—as if anyone could hear over all the noise. "Don't look now, but that guy in the next lane is checking you out, Monica."

Monica turned her head, catching the man in the act. After a brief hesitation, he waved and gave a slow, confident grin. As soon as she smiled back, he sauntered over.

Bridget elbowed Emily. "What'd I tell you."

"Hello, ladies," the man said. "I'm Bart." He looked at Monica. "And you are?"

"Monica. These are my friends, Bridget and Emily."

Bart nodded, then returned his attention to Monica. "I like the way you bowl. That hip thing is something else."

Monica blushed. "I don't know where I learned that. It's just what I do."

"It's cute, but it cuts down on the effectiveness of the ball. I could teach you how to fix that."

"I'm up," Emily announced, but Monica and Bart were too busy making eyes at each other to pay her any attention.

Emily bowled a spare. Bridget clapped and whooped. "Way to go, Em!"

"When you're hot, you're hot." Laughing, Emily blew on her fingers and rubbed them against her upper chest.

That caught Monica's attention. "I should get back to my friends," she said.

Bart nodded. "Nice meeting you ladies." He pointed at Monica. "I'll talk to you later." He ambled off.

"Just look at him," she murmured. "I love ranchers— all muscle, no fat. He asked for my number." She looked pleased with herself.

"And you obviously gave it to him. I would've, too." Bridget let out a sigh. "I so envy you, and I'm darned tired of being single. You're up again, Monica."

Emily wasn't envious. Liking a guy, wanting him to like her, waiting for him to call, then getting disappointed or hurt... Who needed that?

For a while, she and her friends bowled and laughed and forgot all about men. They were on the last frame and talking about calling it an early night, when Bridget whistled softly. "There goes my idea of the perfect man. Too bad he has a date, because for him, I'd be willing to flirt like Monica."

Emily followed her friend's gaze. To her surprise, she saw Seth Pettit. What was he doing here?

His arm was around an attractive woman who looked vaguely familiar. His head was bent toward her while she animatedly talked. Taylor and another gorgeous man about Seth's age accompanied them. For all Seth's words the other night about having too much on his plate to date, it appeared that he had a girlfriend. That had happened fast—he hadn't lived here that long.

Yet he'd kissed Emily as if he meant business. Then a couple of days ago, when she'd driven Taylor home, he'd looked at her like he wanted to do it again.

Emily wasn't sure what bothered her most—the lie, the kiss, the *I'm interested* heat in his eyes or the fact that her pulse rate bumped up at the sight of him.

Suddenly Seth glanced her way, almost as if he felt her gaze. His eyes widened. He said something to his girlfriend, then flashed Emily a heart-stopping grin and steered the woman toward her.

Refusing to smile at the dirty bum, she crossed her arms over her chest.

Chapter Eight

For reasons undetermined, Emily eyed Seth coolly and then dismissed him altogether. She sure wasn't happy to see him.

Puzzled, he took his arm from around his sister. "Hey, there. Didn't expect to run into you."

"Hello, Seth," she replied in a voice as aloof as her expression. "Hi, Taylor."

"Emily!" To Seth's astonishment, Taylor's lips curled into the closest thing to a smile he'd seen since he'd taken custody of her. "What are you doing here?"

"Bowling with a couple of girlfriends—or trying." Her laugh seemed force and excluded him. "None of us is very good. Seth and Taylor, meet Monica and Bridget."

At least her two friends smiled. The short one with the sassy black hair fluttered her eyelashes. He wasn't impressed. Wasn't interested in the tall redhead, either.

Emily was the one he wanted. She was the prettiest woman in the place. Her pale yellow sweater clung softly to her breasts, and dark jeans hugged her sweet behind. Seth wanted to grab hold and pull her close. Not that he would, even if they were alone.

Because right now, she looked as if she'd rather drop a bowling ball on her foot than be standing there, talking to him. He had no clue why she was giving him the cold shoulder.

"Since my brother seems to have forgotten I'm here, I'll introduce myself," his companion said. "I'm Dani, and this is my husband, Nick."

"Ah, you're Seth's sister." Some of the starch went out of Emily's spine. "I thought you were his date."

She'd been jealous. Well, well. Seth liked that a little too much. He fought to hide his grin, then gave himself a mental kick in the butt. As attracted as he was to Emily, he was not going to get involved with her.

"It's nice to meet you both." Emily smiled. "I'm Emily Miles."

"The woman who owns The Wagging Tail," Nick said.

Emily looked surprised. "You've heard of us?"

"On the drive over, Taylor only mentioned it and you half a dozen times."

Taylor blushed furiously and frowned, but Nick gave her a teasing smile that seemed to coax her into relaxing. Seth envied his brother-in-law. Taylor never let him off that easily.

"Have we met?" Dani asked Emily.

Emily frowned. "Not that I know of, but I think I've seen you around."

"Do you ever eat at Big Mama's Café?"

"I used to go a lot, but not since I started the shelter. Did we meet there?"

"You might have," Seth said. "Dani owns Big Mama's."

Clearly proud, she beamed. "Actually, I own it with my mom. She's retired now, but she started the business over forty years ago."

"Your mom is Big Mama?" Emily was impressed.

Dani laughed. "That's right. She used to be my foster mom, and then I got really lucky—she adopted me."

"Lucky is right," Emily said. "My mother's idea of cooking is to open a prepackaged meal and warm it up. Big Mama's a wonderful cook. Those cinnamon rolls…" Just thinking about them, Emily groaned.

Everyone in the group echoed her, which made Dani laugh again. These days, almost everything did. She was that happy.

"She doesn't make those anymore and neither do I, but we have a couple of great chefs."

In the silence that fell, Seth turned to Emily. "I didn't know you were into bowling."

"As you can see from my ratty, rented shoes, I'm not. I freely admit that I really suck at it." She didn't look at all upset about that.

"We're all terrible at bowling," the woman with the reddish hair agreed with a laugh.

Seth couldn't help but smile. "I'm not great, either, but I needed a night out."

He'd been about to bust out of his skin with restlessness, needing to do something on a Saturday night besides paperwork, dealing with Taylor and watching the tube. Having gone too long without sex didn't help, either.

If he'd been alone this evening, he would have headed for a bar to have a beer and maybe meet a willing woman. Living with a surly teenage girl didn't allow for that. Especially when she had no friends and nothing on her agenda. Staying home had seemed the right thing to do.

"Dani and Nick called tonight and invited Taylor and me along. Taylor said okay, and I figured, why not?" Seth was pleased that she'd wanted to come.

"I had no idea she was a bowler until tonight," he went on. "I'm counting on you to give me some tips," he said to Taylor, and placed his hand on her shoulder.

"I don't bowl anymore," she muttered, moving quickly out of reach.

That stung. Would she never let him give her affection?

Emily's sympathetic gaze took in both him and Taylor. "What made you stop?" she asked.

Taylor hung her head. "It was something I used to do with my mom."

Everyone sobered up at that. Seth's chest hurt for her. "I didn't know," he said.

"Because you didn't ask."

Feeling even worse, he shifted his weight. "Would you rather we leave?"

"We're here now. We may as well stay."

"That's the spirit." Emily gave Taylor a thumbs-up. "I know that wherever your mom is, she's smiling at you right now."

A guilty expression flitted across Taylor's face. What was that about?

"While you're here, be sure to order some fries from the food counter," Emily said. "They're yummy."

"Oh, we will." Dani smacked her lips. "That's one of the reasons I dragged everyone here tonight."

"That's my Dani." Nick put his arm around her and kissed her lightly on the lips. They'd been married two years, and every time Seth saw them they still acted like honeymooners.

"Taylor, did you ask about the fund-raiser pizza party?" Emily asked.

Without so much as a glance Seth's way, she nodded. "I can come."

Emily's face lit in a smile. "That's terrific. Will you be joining us, too, Seth?"

"That depends on Taylor," he said carefully.

"I don't want you there."

"Ouch," he muttered, none too softly.

"But I do." Emily glanced at him. "You know animals so well, and I'm sure you have some great ideas on how to raise money for our shelter."

"I don't know…" Taylor bit her lip.

"Think it over."

Seth appreciated that Emily was letting the kid make up her own mind. If he'd had more of a chance to do that when he was growing up, life would have been easier for everyone.

The announcement came over the loudspeaker. "Pettit, party of four, lane twelve is ready for you."

"Have fun," Emily said.

He nodded. "I emailed that questionnaire back this afternoon. If you want to get together and talk about my website, I have time on Monday."

Her gaze met his, and then skittered away, as if staring into his eyes was dangerous. With so much heat between them, it was definitely dangerous.

"We don't actually need a face-to-face meeting," she said. "I'll look over your answers, and we'll go from there."

"Suit yourself. Good night, ladies."

Emily and her friends headed off.

"So that's the 'famous' Emily Miles," Dani commented as the three women left. "I see why you like her, Taylor. She's pretty cool. Hey, Nick, why don't you and Taylor get the fries. Seth and I will meet you at our lane."

His sister hooked arms with him and they headed off. "There's something between you and Emily," she said, with a canny look.

"Uh, yeah. I'm the volunteer vet at her shelter, and she's letting Taylor do her community service there."

"I mean something more."

"Like what?"

"There's a pretty obvious attraction between you two."

True, but that was none of his sister's business.

"But it's more than that," Dani went on. "You seem to really like each other."

She was enjoying her life, which was great. But she tended to see the world through rose-colored glasses.

"Just because you're happy and in love doesn't mean everyone else should be," Seth said. She opened her mouth, but he cut her off. "Let's bowl."

"When you told us about Seth, you forgot to mention that he's drop-dead gorgeous," Monica said as she, Emily and Bridget exited the bowling alley. "Is he seeing anyone?"

Bridget scrutinized Emily. "From the way he looked

at you, I'd guess that he'd like to be seeing *you*. I'll bet if he asked you out, you'd get interested in dating real fast."

Emily *was* interested, and running into Seth tonight had only confirmed that. Her feelings scared her. She wasn't about to risk getting involved with him. "He is attractive," she hedged. "But he's getting his practice off the ground and has his hands full with Taylor. You saw how she was with him. He doesn't have time for anything else, and neither do I."

Monica scoffed. "If that's what he told you, he's changed his mind. The way he looked at you... Whew." She fanned herself.

Emily knew she was blushing, and felt relieved that the scant light from the parking lot concealed the fact. "I'm riding shotgun," she called out.

"Back to what you said about not having time to date," Monica said, while Bridget eased out of the parking space. "No one can work all the time, not even you. Hanging out with us now and then isn't enough. You need to get a life."

"That's right," Bridget said. "Two words—Aunt Arlene."

Emily rolled her eyes. "FYI, I *do* have a life, and it's pretty full. And there's nothing wrong with spending an occasional evening with my BFFs. Bowling was a hoot, and don't forget our great greasy food fest. In my book, that's good livin'."

"It was fun," Monica agreed. "But I wouldn't mind getting some of my kicks with a sexy man." She blew out a breath. "I don't think it will be with Seth Pettit, though. He's all about you."

"For sure." Bridget glanced at her. "What are you afraid of, Em?"

"I'm not afraid," she insisted. Then sighed. "I guess I am a little wary of getting hurt again. The men I care about tend not to stick around."

"You can't judge all guys based on what Harvey did,"

Monica said. "He's a stupid jerk. And anyway, we're talking dating here, not falling in love or getting engaged."

She had a point.

"If Seth asks you out, promise you'll go," she went on.

Bridget pulled up Emily's driveway. "Thanks for the ride," Emily said, reaching for the passenger door.

"Not so fast." Monica poked her. "What about Seth?"

Emily turned around in her seat so that she could see her friend. "He isn't going to ask me out. But if he does, I'll think about it. Okay? I'll talk to you soon."

Chapter Nine

Monday morning, Emily sat in her office, nursing her coffee and reading through the questionnaire Seth had answered and emailed back. She'd printed it out, and as she reviewed his comments, it was obvious that he'd given his website some thought and knew what he wanted.

A decisive guy who liked animals and had made a commitment to finish raising a girl he wasn't related to made Seth Pettit a one-of-a-kind man. Who, according to Monica and Bridget, was interested in her. What was Emily supposed to do about that? She didn't want his interest—at least not the rational part of her.

Suddenly, the shelter doorbell rang. Susannah woofed and stood up. It wasn't even eight o'clock yet, and Emily wasn't expecting anyone. The shelter didn't open until nine, but from time to time, people showed up unannounced to discuss adopting a dog, or to drop one off.

Before answering the door, she shut her pet in the office. "I'm not taking any chances of exposing you to a contagious disease," she explained. "I'll be back as soon as I can to let you out."

Wondering what to expect, she opened the door.

To her surprise, Seth stood there.

"Hey," he said, holding up a white bakery box bearing the Big Mama's Café logo.

The unmistakable aroma of cinnamon rolls still warm from the oven made Emily's mouth water. "Cinnamon rolls. Wow." Her stomach gurgled in anticipation. "I've been wanting one of those since Saturday night. How did you know?"

"Because I have, too. We're lucky that even though the restaurant is closed on Mondays, they sell these. Got any coffee?"

"As a matter of fact, I do. Come in."

When Seth entered the room, Susannah woofed from Emily's office.

"I put her in there in case you were someone dropping off a stray," she said. "I'll go and let her out."

"I'll come with." Seth shrugged out of his parka. "We can eat these while we discuss my website."

"You didn't have to drive all the way over here, Seth. I told you the other night, we can easily do this by email or phone."

"If possible, I want to nail down the design today. As busy as we both are, now seems like the perfect time." His eyes sparkling with humor, he held up the bakery box.

She laughed. "Bribing me with cinnamon rolls will get you pretty much anything. It just so happens that I was looking over your answers when you showed up. Let's get our coffee, and then do this."

Emily opened her office door. Woofing happily, Susannah hurried to Seth's side and nosed his hand for a rub. He didn't disappoint. He set the box in the center of her desk, where the dog couldn't reach it, and then accompanied Emily to the kitchen. Within minutes, they returned to her office with plates, napkins and steaming mugs.

Seth sat across the desk from her. Emily bit into a cinnamon roll, closed her eyes and moaned in ecstasy.

When she opened them, he was studying her with a hooded look that went straight to her belly. Her nerves began to hum, and for a few moments she forgot all about the bakery treat. Hastily glancing away, she pushed the questionnaire across the desk and asked for clarification on one of his answers. Seth explained, and they moved on to other comments.

"Since you're here, let's check out some of the sites you listed that have features you want," she said.

Seth pulled his chair around next to hers so that they could both see the computer screen. Between his comments and her input, she managed to get a clear idea of his vision.

"I have everything I need now," she said when they'd finished. "Over the next few days, I'll put together a prototype and send you a link. You tell me what you like and don't like about it, and I'll make adjustments from there."

"Great."

Instead of moving his chair around the desk again, he left it beside hers, which was a little unnerving. She sat back, distancing herself a little. "Did Taylor enjoy bowling?"

"I couldn't tell." He glanced at her mouth and frowned.

"What?" she said.

"You have something right there." He touched his finger to his own mouth. "It looks like icing from the cinnamon roll."

Emily licked the spot with the tip of her tongue. "Did I get it?"

Seth cleared his throat. "Not quite."

He leaned in and rubbed the spot with his finger. "See?" He held it out to her.

He was so close, she could see the silvery flecks that made his blue eyes so interesting. Make that mesmerizing. She couldn't look away.

Without thinking, she licked his finger clean.

He let out a low, masculine growl. "I know you want more than I can give, and I keep telling myself to stay away from you. But I can't resist you."

What did he mean, she wanted more than he could give?

Emily wondered. She would find out later. Right now, there were more important things on the agenda. She leaned in and met him halfway.

EMILY TASTED OF cinnamon rolls, coffee and her own sweet self. Seth lost himself in a kiss that left him hungry for more. Needing to touch her, he ran his hands up her slender back. She was small-boned and delicate, yet also strong, with an eagerness that matched his.

Need hit him hard—emphasis on *hard*. He wanted her.

He skimmed his hands up her sides, to her breasts. She went still and inched back, silently granting him the access he wanted. Her breasts filled his palms, all warm and soft. She moaned right into his mouth.

His body on fire, Seth kissed her again, this time more deeply. Her tongue tangled restlessly with his. He wanted her naked, wanted inside her.

He was easing her back against the desk when Susannah woofed and the latch to the front door clicked.

Emily jerked away and shot a startled glance at the clock. "It's nine o'clock. That's Mrs. Oakes."

She tugged down her sweater. Tucked her hair behind her ears. But nothing could erase the thoroughly kissed, pink plumpness of her mouth.

Seth swallowed hard. He didn't move. Couldn't. "I'd better not stand up right now," he said, with a wry look at his erection.

"Oh." Emily's eyes widened. "Just scoot your chair back around the desk and try to look busy."

He complied. All business, she stared at the computer screen in studied concentration.

"Morning," Mrs. Oakes called from the front room.

"Good morning," Emily replied.

"Hey, Mrs. Oakes," Seth said.

His voice brought her into the office. "Well, hello," she cooed, a warm smile following her curious expression. "I swear it feels like winter today. But it's nice and warm in here."

Emily blushed. "Seth and I are working on his website. He brought cinnamon rolls from Big Mama's. There's one for you, in the kitchen."

"For me?" Mrs. Oakes beamed. "You're a keeper, Seth Pettit."

He wasn't used to that kind of talk, and it made him uncomfortable. "I'm just a guy with a sweet tooth," he said.

Emily was sweet enough to satisfy his craving for sugar. As if she read his mind, her gaze connected with his and held. Seth wanted badly to kiss her again. With Mrs. Oakes hovering around, it wasn't going to happen.

He slid his chair back. "I'd better go. There's a horse with a rotten tooth waiting for me. But first, I'll check on the dog with mange. I'll let myself into the quarantine hut. Catch you later."

OVER THE NEXT few days, Emily placed the German shepherd and a golden retriever mix in new homes. She barely had time to let out a breath of relief before a new dog arrived early Thursday morning. He was waiting in quarantine for Seth to examine him.

As soon as Mrs. Oakes returned from lunch, Emily left to pick up dog food and other supplies. Despite the sun, the temperature hovered just above freezing, and when she returned an hour later with her purchases, her hands stung from the cold.

After placing her purse and a case of dog biscuits on Mrs. Oakes's desk, she blew on her fists. "I should've worn gloves. While I bring in the rest of the supplies, would you mind opening this box and setting aside a package of treats for you know who?"

She didn't fool Susannah. Tongue out and tail wagging, she obviously knew exactly what was in the box.

"Will do," Mrs. Oakes said. "You just missed Seth. He seemed sorry that you weren't here."

Emily was both relieved and disappointed. Although she wanted to see him, she needed time to pull herself together. Not so easy, with the constant fantasies she was having. Fantasies that involved the two of them. She could almost feel his hungry mouth on hers again, and his hands on her breasts...

Just the thought made her nipples tighten.

It was bad enough that she wanted him. Worse still, she liked him. *Really* liked him, way more than was wise.

Mrs. Oakes was giving her a curious look, and she busied herself opening the box she'd just asked the office manager to open. "What did he say about the new dog?"

"First, good news! He checked on the female with mange again. She's almost ready to move into the kennel. He phoned in a couple of prescriptions for the new dog, and left a note on your desk. You're supposed to call with any questions. I hope you'll come up with some. You need to contact that man."

Clearly, the woman wanted Emily and Seth the get together, but for so many reasons, it just wasn't a good idea. "If I have any, I'll ask when he picks up Taylor this afternoon. I'd better bring in the rest of the supplies."

"Need any help?"

"You're not supposed to lift heavy things," Emily reminded her. Mrs. Oakes had problems with her back, and the last thing either of them needed was for her to wind up home in bed while pulled muscles healed. "But feel free to give you know who a you know what."

Emily drove around to the rear of the building. While she shelved the food and stacked new bedding and other supplies, she went back to thinking about Seth, and why what they were doing was dangerous.

If the kisses and more that they'd started continued and escalated, the shelter could be jeopardized. Seth had agreed to stay through the semester, but he could always change his mind. Emily wanted him to stay on indefinitely. She certainly didn't want to push him the other way.

Even riskier, if her feelings for him continued to grow... Scared by the very idea, Emily firmly pushed the thought away. She wouldn't *let* them grow. She didn't have the time for a relationship, and neither did Seth.

Never mind that they both seemed to have the time and interest to fool around.

Remembering the feel of his hands on her breasts while they shared delicious kisses, she went all soft inside. But when he changed his mind and grew tired of her—what then? Because that was what men did, at least the men in Emily's life. One day they loved you, and the next, they were gone.

The smartest and safest thing to do was to stay focused on the reason Seth had come into her life in the first place— to care for the dogs. For the sake of them and the shelter, she wouldn't kiss or be alone with him again.

There was only one little problem. Now that her body was awake, she wanted more. So much more.

No, she told herself. Just *no.* Resolved, she put the last of the supplies away.

EMILY WAS SURPRISED when Taylor and Cat entered the shelter together. This time they'd both dressed for the weather in coats, jeans and boots.

No longer cautious or reticent, they chatted animatedly, and once or twice, Taylor even laughed. Seth would be pleased.

"Lots of news," Emily told them. "The two dogs you girls walked last week have both found permanent homes. We took in a new male this morning, and Seth has already been here to check him out. He seems to be in reasonably good shape. And the dog with mange is almost ready to move into the kennel."

As soon as Taylor heard Seth's name, she grimaced.

Why did she dislike him so much? Emily wanted to ask, but not in front of Cat or Mrs. Oakes. "Today I'd like you to walk two other dogs," she said. "Then Taylor, you'll input the data about the new arrival into our computer database, and Cat, you'll launder the new towels and blankets I bought today."

Several hours later, while the girls waited for their rides home, Emily reminded them about the fund-raiser party. "See you tomorrow night, right?" she asked.

Both girls nodded.

"Is everyone from community service going?" Cat asked.

"Matt and Shayna have that football game and can only come for a little while, but everyone else will be staying until the meeting ends. Seven adult volunteers will also be here."

"My parents are coming with me," Cat said. "Are you bringing Seth, Taylor? He sounds cool and I want to meet him."

What would Taylor say? Emily didn't move a muscle.

"He's coming, but only because Emily invited him," the girl said.

Cat grinned. "Epic." Current slang for *really cool*. "Taylor, have you seen the dog getting a bath on Vine?"

"No. Show it to me."

Cat fiddled with her phone, then beckoned Emily over. "You should see this, too—it's hilarious."

Watching two teenage boys wrestle with a reluctant animal and get drenched, Emily laughed as heartily as the girls.

Cat was putting her phone away when a car horn beeped. She peered out the window. "There's my mom. See you tomorrow night. I'll text you, Taylor."

"It's great that you and Cat are getting along so well," Emily said as the door closed behind her.

"We have to work together, so we may as well." Taylor shrugged, as if making a friend was no big deal. "Seth just pulled up. Bye."

As she exited the building, her whole demeanor changed. Her shoulders slumped and her footsteps got heavier.

Emily had the feeling the downcast manner was for Seth's benefit. Could it be that she wanted him to think she was more unhappy than she actually was?

Chapter Ten

"You don't have to come tonight," Taylor said, as Seth pulled the truck into the small parking area of The Wagging Tail. Not counting Emily's car, there were close to a dozen vehicles already there. "I mean, if you'd rather go out or something."

Seth shook his head. "I told Emily I'd be here. I'm looking forward to this."

Not the meeting—seeing Emily. They'd exchanged emails about his website, but he hadn't talked to or laid eyes on her since Monday morning. It almost felt as if she was avoiding him. Nah. She was as busy as he was—that was all.

"Why are you *really* here?" Taylor asked, giving him her tough-girl look.

If they hadn't spent over a month under the same roof, he would have missed the vulnerability buried under her hard expression. "What are you getting at?" he said.

"You're spying on me, and I don't like it."

Now he was confused. Did she really think he was here to watch her every move? He snorted. "I have no reason to spy on you, Taylor, not tonight or ever. You're a good kid."

"If you think I believe you…"

He'd barely set the parking brake before she jumped out of the pickup, her coltish legs eating up the space between the truck and the front door.

Teenage girls. He'd never understand them.

When he entered the office, Mrs. Oakes was collecting

her purse and shrugging into her coat. "Now that you're here, I can lock up and go home," she said.

"You waited for us?" Seth asked.

She nodded. "You're the last ones."

Taylor glared at him. "We're late because of you."

"Would you rather I left a calf with a barbwire gash on her back to fend for herself?"

"No, but... Forget it."

Mrs. Oakes gave Seth a sympathetic look. "Will the calf be all right?"

"Now that I cleaned her up and treated her, she will."

"That's good. The stairs to Emily's apartment are behind the kitchen. There's a big group up there. Have fun, and both of you have a good weekend."

"You, too, Mrs. Oakes." Taylor smiled at the woman before she headed for the stairs.

At least she was civil to other people.

She didn't utter another word to him. Emily's apartment door was open a fraction and voices filled the air.

As if Seth were invisible, Taylor walked in ahead of him.

The small living room was crowded with teens and a dozen or so adults, and smelled like fresh-baked pizza that made his mouth water. On one side of the room, several large pies filled a table.

Emily's hair was loose and wavy, and she was dressed in flowing, silky-looking pants and a matching top that was both feminine and sexy.

"You made it."

Her smile encompassed both of them and transformed her from pretty to beautiful. Seth didn't hide his appreciation. Flushing, she glanced away.

"Put your coats in the bedroom down the hall, then make yourself a name tag and help yourself to pizza and pop."

Before Seth had shrugged out of his jacket, Taylor tossed him hers and again separated from him.

He gave Emily a what-can-you-do look.

"We need to talk later," she said, in a voice for his ears only.

Wondering what she wanted to talk about, he headed for the bedroom. Her apartment was old and small, but she'd made it homey with colorful throw rugs and interesting dog photos on the hallway wall.

He added his and Taylor's coats to the pile on the bed. The room was barely big enough for the queen-size bed. Seth couldn't help but imagine the two of them, lying there together...

"Excuse me, everyone," Emily said over the noise.

He quickly rejoined the group, stopping to print his name on a name tag and slap it on his chest.

"Help yourselves to pizza and something to drink, and please introduce yourselves to each other. My student volunteers have all met, but the adults don't know you and some don't know each other. Let me quickly introduce my adult volunteers to all of you. Over there are Caroline, Janice, Patty and Lester, the angels who bring the dogs to the shelter, walk them in the morning and do whatever else is needed. Barb and Irene are great at stepping in whenever they can. Last but definitely not least, Seth Pettit, the tall man heading toward the pizza table, is our amazing volunteer veterinarian."

People looked at him and murmured in appreciation. Uncomfortable being singled out, Seth gave a modest nod.

Before he made it to the pizza, a teenage girl with heavily made-up eyes, a friendly smile and artsy-looking clothes, waylaid him, Taylor reluctantly following.

"I'm Cat, Taylor's friend," she said. "Thanks for taking care of the shelter dogs."

He smiled. "Any friend of Taylor's is a friend of mine. Nice to meet you."

With a mortified expression, Taylor pulled on her friend's arm. "Let's find a place to sit."

As they moved away, Seth took his place at the end of the line. As soon as he helped himself to pizza, he looked for a place to sit. Emily had set out folding chairs, but the kids had ignored them in favor of the floor.

Sitting cross-legged against the wall, Taylor and Cat were carrying on an animated conversation. He'd never seen Taylor without the sullen look. She chattered away, punctuating the conversation with smiles, just as the nine-year-old girl he remembered once had. She'd finally made a friend. Relieved, he grinned to himself. Maybe now she'd accept that Prosperity was her home.

He found a seat beside several parents, most of whom looked to be around his age.

He introduced himself all around and was pleased to learn that the couple beside him were Cat's parents.

"I met Cat earlier," he said. "She and Taylor have become friends. She seems warm and outgoing."

Her father laughed. "Unless she's in one of her moods."

Seth shook his head. "I know exactly what you mean."

"I understand you and Taylor are from San Diego," Cat's mother said.

Seth was surprised that she knew about that. Taylor must have told Cat. "Taylor is," he corrected. "I'm from Sacramento, but I was born here in Prosperity."

"You and Taylor are from different cities?" Cat's father looked confused.

This wasn't the time or place to get into that. "It's a long story I don't want to get into right now," Seth said.

Suddenly Susannah bounded into the room with her odd gait. Emily snapped her fingers, and the whippet moved to her side. A moment later she trotted over and greeted Seth with a wagging tail and a pleading look.

"Hey, girl," he said, patting her. "I didn't bring any dog biscuits with me tonight." Undaunted, the animal trotted off in search of a snack from someone else.

Emily moved to the front of the room, near an easel that had been set up. "That's Susannah, and she's looking for food," she said over the noise. "Don't give her any."

Matt and Shayna exchanged *uh-oh* looks. "Um, we just did," Shayna said.

Emily didn't seem too upset. "It's not your fault. When she looks at you with those big brown eyes, she's pretty hard to resist."

Low chuckles filled the room.

"Matt and Shayna have a football game tonight and will be leaving soon, so we should start our meeting," Emily said. "Every year I host a fund-raiser so that The Wagging Tail can continue operating. When I first started accepting high school kids for community service three years ago, I realized what a valuable resource you all are. During our brainstorming session tonight I'm calling on your creativity." She paused to smile.

"All right, let's get started. Who has ideas for this year's fund-raiser?" Several hands went up. "You don't have to raise your hands," she said. "Just call out your ideas."

"Sell candy," Jessie said.

Emily wrote it down. "What else?"

Kids and adults began to call out suggestions.

"Sell magazine subscriptions."

"Write a story about The Wagging Tail, put it in the school paper and ask for donations."

"Hold a silent auction."

"Have a car wash."

"Host a bake sale."

The ideas had petered out when Matt and Shayna stood to leave, along with Matt's mother. *"Sorry,"* the woman mouthed.

"No problem. I'm glad you made it." Emily smiled at the teens. "See you two next week. I'll let you know what we decided then."

Twenty minutes later, the group had pared down the list of ideas to a silent auction, stories in the high school paper from the schools represented—articles to be vetted by Emily before submission—and asking a reporter to write an article for the *Prosperity Daily News*.

"Now we need to find companies willing to donate to the silent auction," Emily said. "Who wants to solicit our local businesses?"

Every kid volunteered for that job. They discussed where to go for donations, and divided up various business areas. Taylor and Cat asked for a section of downtown.

When the meeting ended, Seth was surprised that several hours had passed.

Wondering what Emily wanted to talk to him about, he hung around until only he and Taylor remained.

"Let's go," she said.

"First I need to talk to Emily."

"About what?"

He raised his eyebrows at Emily. "You heard the girl."

She fiddled with her hoop earring. "We don't have to talk tonight," she said. "It can wait."

Too curious for that, Seth shook his head. "Let's do it now."

Emily glanced at Taylor. "Do you mind waiting a little longer to leave?"

"Whatever." She pulled her phone from her pocket. "I'll be in the office."

As her footsteps echoed down the steps, Seth turned to Emily.

WITH EVERYONE BUT Seth gone, Emily's living room should have felt bigger. But he somehow made it seem even smaller. For some reason, standing there in her apartment and explaining that the kissing had to stop seemed dangerous. Plus, after a long day and busy evening, she was tired.

"I enjoyed tonight," Seth said, his eyes warm. "You're a natural at conducting a meeting."

"Thanks, but what really matters is how much money the fund-raiser brings in."

"How much are you looking to raise?"

She gave him a number. "That's what we need to keep the clinic running for another year. And it would be nice to be able to pay you and some of our other volunteers something."

"You know I could use the money," Seth said. "But watching Taylor laugh and enjoy herself—that's the best payment of all. I hardly recognized her."

"Credit her friendship with Cat for that. They seem to really like each other."

"But without you, they wouldn't have met." He glanced at the overflowing wastebasket and cluttered table. "I'll give you a hand with this stuff."

If only he wouldn't look at her with those heated eyes… He made her want things she shouldn't, dangerous things that could put the shelter at risk and leave her with a broken heart.

"Emily?" Seth gave her a funny look. "I said, where do you want me to put the trash?"

"There's a bin behind the building. I'll take it out later. You already gave up a big chunk of your evening and you offered a free animal exam for the silent auction," she said. "That's enough. Besides, Taylor is waiting downstairs."

"She won't mind. She's probably texting or talking to someone on FaceTime. I'll take the trash down when I leave." He started flattening the folding chairs she'd set up. "Let me put these away. Then you can tell me what you wanted to talk about."

The man wouldn't quit. All right, then they would talk tonight. Emily collapsed two of the folding chairs and hefted them. "The utility closet is off the kitchen. This way."

She led him down the hall, past at least a dozen framed photos of dogs and their new human families.

"You have pictures like these in the other hallway, too," Seth said. "They're nice."

"Every one features a dog from the shelter. After they're adopted, I snap a photo so that I can remember them." Emily opened the accordion door hiding the washer and dryer. "In here."

When they returned to the living room, Seth eyed her expectantly. It was time for that talk. She gestured for him to sit on the couch, and plunked down on the coffee table across from him.

Their knees were almost touching, which was distracting. She slid the table back a little and, suddenly nervous, brushed an imaginary thread from her sleeve. "The other morning, you said something about me wanting more than you can give. What did you mean?"

"Is that what you wanted to talk about? I meant that you're not a casual relationship kind of woman, but I don't have time for anything else. I hardly even have time for that."

He was right—she wasn't into casual flings. On the other hand, assuming she might want something serious when she didn't… Determined to set him straight, Emily folded her arms. "I don't happen to want a serious relationship just now." She pushed an image of Bridget's aunt Arlene, with her pinched expression, from her mind. "Relationships take a lot of time and work, and there are too many other things to worry about."

"Exactly." Seth blew out a breath that sounded like relief. "Good to know we're on the same page."

"Along those lines, I don't think we should be kissing each other," Emily added.

"Probably not. But when I'm with you, I don't always think straight."

He glanced at her lips, sending a rush of longing through her. "I'm the same way," she admitted. "When I'm around you, I…" How to explain? She swallowed. "I've never experienced this…this *feeling* with any other man."

"It's called animal magnetism, and we sure have it."

At the moment, his eyes were more silver than blue, and bright with desire. "It doesn't help that you have the sexiest mouth on the planet."

She did?

"When I see you, I want to touch those lips." He leaned forward and ran this thumb across her bottom one.

Her mouth automatically opened a fraction, and he made a pleased sound. "You're such a responsive woman. I want to taste you, claim you."

That intimate, low voice… Every nerve in her body shivered with longing.

Then footsteps sounded on the stairs.

"That's Taylor," Seth muttered, dropping his hand.

Emily's eyes opened—they'd drifted shut without her realizing it. She jumped up and smoothed her silk tunic. "This is why we shouldn't be alone together anymore."

"It's probably safer that way." Seth gave her one last hungry look then grabbed two bulging plastic trash bags.

Taylor entered the room, her eyes narrowing. Did she suspect that Emily had been about to go up in flames?

"What's taking so long?" she asked.

"We were cleaning up and talking about the fund-raiser," Seth replied, as if nothing was amiss. "How about giving me a hand with these?"

Downstairs, Emily waited for them to dispose of the trash and leave so that she could lock up. "Good night, and thank you both for coming and for helping me clean up," she said.

She didn't relax until she turned the dead bolt and heard Seth's truck purr down the driveway.

Chapter Eleven

Late afternoon on the first Sunday in October, Seth headed with Taylor to Sly and Lana's. Normally, his brother and sister-in-law had Sunday dinner at Lana's parents' house, but not tonight. As usual, Taylor had her earbuds in, leaving Seth to his own thoughts.

At the moment, they centered on his brother. They hadn't seen each other or spoken since Seth had delivered the twin calves a couple weeks earlier. But Seth thought about him often, wondering how to close the huge cavern that separated them, or if that was even possible.

Take tonight's invitation, which had come from Lana, not Sly. At first, Seth had been reluctant to accept. Who needed another uncomfortable evening? But Dani and Nick were also coming, with big news of some kind. Whatever it was, Dani wanted Seth to hear it from her. He'd missed so much family stuff, he figured he'd better show up.

Over the last few hours, the temperature had dropped to below freezing, and clouds had gathered in the darkening sky.

Taylor hugged herself and pulled her long legs under her. Despite her winter parka, she looked cold. And yet she didn't so much as touch the truck's heat controls. When she wasn't giving him dirty, sullen looks, she seemed overly timid, almost as if she was afraid that she might somehow disappoint him.

The huge contrast confused and really bothered him. It was weird, too. His only disappointment was her continued dislike of him and everything he did and said. Although, since the meeting at Emily's last Friday, she'd become somewhat more talkative.

Seth wondered what she'd think if she knew that he lusted over Emily. Since their talk, they'd made a point of never being in the same place without someone else present, but that didn't curb his desire for her. Not being able to touch or kiss her only made his hunger stronger, to the point that he fantasized about her all the time. He needed a woman and soon, or he just might explode.

"Feel free to crank up the heat," he said, raising his voice so that she'd hear him over whatever she was listening to.

She pulled off the earbuds, fussed with the temperature and directed the heat vents on the passenger side toward her feet. "It's cold."

"Trust me, soon it'll be a lot colder," he said.

"That's what Emily said. When Cat and I were texting earlier, she said it could snow tonight. I didn't think that happened until November."

"In central Montana, you never know. Once, when I was a kid, we got a foot of the stuff in September."

"Epic."

"You aren't kidding." He made a mental note to pick up a sled.

Taylor pulled off her earbuds. "Can I go to Cat's for an overnight?"

Pleased that the girl had invited her over, Seth readily agreed. "If you want to. When are you thinking?"

"Friday night."

"Sure. I'll drive you over."

The ranch was just ahead. He signaled and slowed, then turned at the Pettit Ranch sign. The pickup trundled up the long gravel driveway to the house. He didn't see Dani and Nick's truck, or Sly's, for that matter.

By the time he parked and climbed out, Taylor was on her way to the front door.

Lana opened it. Johanna, who was almost four, ran to

greet her. Mark, age fourteen months, toddled forward. Taylor gave them both hugs. She was good with them.

"Hi, you two," Lana said. She kissed Seth's cheek and then hugged Taylor.

"Hey, Lana." Taylor accepted the hug and returned it.

Seth wished he could hug her like that. At least she was nicer to him than she had been.

She went off to play with Johanna, Mark squealing and toddling after them.

Seth handed Lana the flowers he'd picked up at the grocery store. "These are for you."

"Aww, thanks. Come into the kitchen while I find a vase. Dani called," Lana said as he accompanied her down a wide hall to their big, homey kitchen. "She and Nick are running late. Sly's out picking up dessert, so it's just us. How about a beer?"

"Thanks." Seth slid onto a chair at the breakfast bar. "Need any help with dinner?"

She shook her head. "There's nothing left to do but toss the salad. Taylor seems a lot more comfortable than she did the last time she was here."

"She's doing better. Community service at the dog shelter has helped. She made a friend there. She'll be staying at her house Friday night."

A night to himself. Seth hadn't fully digested that yet. He figured he'd go to a bar and look around for a woman, someone to take his mind off Emily. *Yeah, buddy. Good luck with that.*

Before long, Dani, Nick and Sly arrived.

"Look who we ran into as we pulled up the drive," Dani said. She kissed Lana's cheek and gave Seth a sisterly hug and kiss. "Our big brother bought *two* apple pies and a gallon of ice cream for tonight."

Her eyes seemed to sparkle with excitement, making Seth wonder about her and Nick's news.

Seth and Nick warmly clapped each other's shoulders.

But Sly merely nodded at Seth, as if they were acquaintances instead of brothers.

That stung, but what had he expected? Not about to let on, Seth acted as if all was well. "How are those twin calves doing?" he asked.

"So far, so good."

The conversation ended there. To Seth's relief, Lana called the kids and summoned Taylor and the adults to bring the food to the table.

Everyone sat, but before they could dish up, Dani gestured for them to wait. "Nick and I have an announcement to make." Smiling at each other, the couple clasped hands before she went on. "We're expecting."

"No kidding! That's fabulous!" Lana said.

Sly whooped. "About time."

Happy for his little sister and her husband, and pleased to be in on the family's good news, Seth grinned. "Congratulations."

Even Taylor smiled. "Is it a boy or a girl?" she asked.

"It's too early to tell," Nick said.

"Why are you all so happy?" Johanna asked.

"Because you're going to have a new baby cousin," Dani said.

The little girl seemed pleased. "I want to meet my cousin right now!"

"You can't until— When is your due date?" Lana asked.

"Early March." Dani beamed.

"In the spring," Lana told her daughter.

"Now that I'm pregnant, I'm always hungry." Dani looked at the food and rubbed her hands together.

Seth and Sly both chuckled.

Dinner was a noisy, happy affair. Seth found himself enjoying the chaos. He liked being here, and questioned why he'd left home all those years ago.

Because he'd been hotheaded and angry with Sly for trying to run his life. Trying to act like their dad when they both knew that he was dead.

What if Taylor felt the same way about him? *Hell.* The insight stunned him, but didn't change the fact that she needed his supervision. At the very least until she turned eighteen. Three whole years away. If things kept going the way they were now, by then he'd probably have aged fifty years.

"I hear you're doing your community service at The Wagging Tail," Lana said to Taylor. "Do you like it?"

"It's a pretty cool place. Emily takes in dogs that have been abandoned. Some have been abused, too. She finds homes for them."

"You volunteer there as the vet, right?" Lana asked Seth.

"That's right, and I agree with Taylor—it's a great place." Thanks to Emily.

"On the first Saturday in November, we're doing a fund-raiser to raise money for the shelter," Taylor went on.

Seth noted the "we," which made it sound as if she were a real part of The Wagging Tail. Emily's doing again. She was something else, and he was beyond grateful to her.

"Sly and I will contribute to that," Lana said.

Sly nodded. "Just tell us where to send the check."

"You can do that," Seth said. "You can also contribute to the silent auction. Do you have anything to donate?"

"I do," Dani said. "One dozen Big Mama cinnamon rolls."

The last time Seth had enjoyed a cinnamon roll had been with Emily, followed by a red-hot kiss. Damn, he wished he'd stop thinking about that.

"I'll donate one week of free day care," Lana offered.

"What can I do?" Nick said. "I don't picture people bidding on touring Kelly Ranch."

Lana and Dani exchanged looks. "That's not a bad idea," Lana said. "I'll bet plenty of people in town would like to experience a day in the life of a rancher."

Dani nodded. "A mini dude ranch experience. Nick, you and Sly could both offer that."

The two men glanced at each other and shrugged. "Why not?" Nick said.

Taylor smiled. "Epic. Emily's going to like all those things."

"Seth mentioned a girl you've made friends with at the shelter," Lana said. "Tell us about her."

After shooting Seth a *how dare you talk about me behind my back* frown, Taylor answered. "Her name is Cat. She's adopted, and she goes to Jupiter High. I'm going to her house Friday night for a sleepover."

She said it as if it were no big deal, but Seth knew how important that night was to her.

"What happens if Emily can't find a home for one of her dogs?" Nick asked.

Taylor frowned. "I don't know. That hasn't happened since I've been there."

"If it happens, it's rare," Seth said. "She's pretty good at placing the animals."

Sly and Lana glanced at each other, and he gave a subtle nod. "Lately we've been talking about getting a dog," she said.

"Can we, Mommy? Really, Daddy?" The little girl began to bounce in her seat and clap her hands. Squealing, Mark joined in.

"You should call Emily right away," Taylor said. "She'll have to come over and check you out, but I'm sure she'll like you. I'll put in a good word for you when I see her on Thursday."

"Sly, aren't you and Nick looking for a fourth to round out your poker table on Friday night?" Lana said. "I'll bet Seth plays."

Sly glanced at Seth, his face unreadable. "You interested?"

So much for heading to a bar Friday night. Seth nodded. "Sure am."

"The game is at Tim Carpenter's ranch, which is adjacent to ours. You can pick me up."

"Tim is my cousin," Lana said. "He and Sly have been playing poker since before we got married."

Sly nodded. "We play for money. Bring a wad of it."

"Will do," Seth said, knowing his brother was too careful with his money to squander much in a poker game. Seth couldn't afford to gamble more than a few dollars, and probably shouldn't even risk that, but he was damned if he'd miss a chance to hang out with his big brother. "I'll bring an empty bag, too, to haul my winnings home."

When Seth and Taylor left an hour later, he was in a great mood. His sister was expecting and the meal together had been less tense than he'd figured.

All in all, it had been a pretty good evening.

EMILY STOOD AT the picture window in the front office, watching fat snowflakes fall to the ground. "Look at that snow come down."

Taylor and Cat crowded in beside her. It had been a rare slow Thursday, so quiet that Mrs. Oakes had left early, and Emily had caught up on a pile of shelter paperwork and finished Seth's website. The girls had walked the dogs and worked on the fund-raiser, finishing with time to spare. Now they were waiting for their rides home.

"As fast and furious as it's falling, I can't believe the forecast is for only an inch or so," Emily said. "It's supposed to melt quickly, too. When the flakes are big like that, it means the temperature is mild."

Taylor's face was pressed to the window, like a young child's. "It was supposed to snow last Sunday, only it didn't. I've never seen actual snow before. It's beautiful."

"Yeah," Cat agreed. "But after awhile, we get pretty

tired of it. Just wait. Hey, if it doesn't melt, maybe we can go sledding or ice skating when you come over tomorrow."

Taylor looked wistful. "I only know how to roller skate. Plus, I don't have any ice skates."

"No worries—I'll teach you," Cat said. "You can borrow my mom's skates. She won't mind."

"So you two are hanging out tomorrow?" Emily commented, pleased that Taylor and Cat's friendship had expanded beyond the shelter or shelter-related activities.

Taylor nodded. "We're having a sleepover."

"We're going to eat pizza and watch movies and stuff," Cat said.

"Great. If you know how to roller skate, Taylor, you should pick up ice skating fairly easily. It's a lot of fun, and so is playing in the snow."

Wanting to take advantage of Taylor's uncharacteristic excitement, Emily hatched an idea. "We still have ten minutes before your rides will be here. Let's go outside and show Taylor what snow is all about. You can come, too, Susannah."

She reached for the dog's sweater and leash, both of which she kept on a hook near the door. With a joyous *woof*, the whippet limp-raced toward her.

After snapping on Susannah's sweater, Emily donned a coat and gloves and her wool hat. The girls did the same, and they headed out.

For a while, Taylor, Cat and Susannah raced around the yard. The dog barked and the girls stuck out their tongues, tasting the snow and laughing. Emily had never heard Taylor laugh before. It was a nice sound. Before long, Cat's mother arrived to pick her up.

"Bye, Emily," Cat called out. "See you tomorrow, Taylor. I'll text you later."

"Okay." Taylor waved.

The snowfall began to taper off. "Do you want to stay out for a while longer?" Emily asked.

"Yeah. This is fun."

"Playing in the snow never gets old. I'm sure I've been doing it since I was a toddler, but my very first memory goes back to when I must've been about three or four. My dad and I built a snowman. I remember that it seemed to take forever to roll the snowballs for the body and head. When we finished, the thing looked huge to me." The good memory of her father was one of a handful she cherished.

"Were you afraid of it?"

Emily laughed. "I don't think so. My dad held me up and helped me press in the rocks I picked for her eyes. Yes, our snowman was actually a snow girl."

Taylor kicked the ground, sending up a cloud of powdery snow. "I never knew my dad."

"Mine left when I was nine. That's almost worse than never knowing who he was."

"I was the same age when Seth walked out on my mom and me."

According to what Seth had told Emily, he hadn't walked out on Taylor. He'd wanted to maintain contact. She barely suppressed her surprise. "Are you sure about that?" she asked.

The girl rolled her eyes. "I was *there*. One morning I went to school. When I came home, he was gone. My mom was so upset that we moved away. He had her cell number, but he never called to say he missed me or that he was sorry, not even once."

"I don't understand," Emily asked. "Why did he leave?"

"Because he didn't want a kid."

Emily frowned. "Did your mom tell you that?"

"She didn't have to."

"You should talk to Seth and see what he has to say about it."

"What for? He'll only lie."

"He doesn't lie." Of that, Emily was sure. "Why would you think that, Taylor?"

"I don't want to talk about him anymore," the girl replied with a stony look. "Hey, is it true that no two snowflakes are alike?"

If she wasn't interested in sharing her thoughts, so be it. But Seth should know about this. Emily doubted Taylor would fill him in, so she would. Taylor wouldn't like it, but the poor man was tearing his hair out, trying to help her adjust to her new life. He needed all the insights he could get.

"That's what I've always heard," she said. "So many snowflakes, each of them unique. It boggles the mind."

Taylor squinted at the flakes gathering on her jacket sleeve. "So far, none of them look the same."

Emily checked her own coat sleeve. "Not a one. They're so pretty and lacy."

"Yeah." Taylor gaped in shock at something on her forearm. Suddenly her face crumpled, as if she was in pain.

Alarmed, Emily hurried to her side. "What's wrong?"

The girl pointed at a snowflake. "This is exactly like the design of the necklace I gave my mom for Christmas last year."

"It's beautiful," Emily said. "She must have loved it."

"She wore it a lot. I gave it to the undertaker and he put it on her in her casket." Taylor bit her lip. "What do you think it means?"

For a moment, Emily considered the question. "I'll bet it's a message from her. She's telling you she's okay and that she loves you."

Taylor's eyes filled, and Emily's heart ached for her. "You miss her, huh?" she said softly.

The girl bit her lip and nodded. Then she wiped her eyes. "I'm cold. I want to go in now."

Inside, Emily removed her outerwear, and hung it up. "You look like you could use a hug."

Looking as if she was barely holding herself together, Taylor held up her hands, keeping Emily at bay. She was still grieving terribly for her mother. Emily mentally added that to the things to share with Seth.

She wanted to talk more, but the phone rang. "I'd better answer that," she said with an apologetic smile.

Taylor barely nodded. Still wearing her coat and hat, she faced the window and stared out into the dusk.

Ten minutes later, Emily disconnected and joined her at the window. "That was Lana. She said that after hearing your rave reviews about The Wagging Tail, she and Sly are interested in adopting a dog."

Taylor brightened a little. "She said she was going to call. She and Sly are nice. So are their kids, Johanna and Mark."

"I guessed that from talking with her. I'm going to their ranch early next week, to meet them and review what's involved in adopting a dog from our shelter. Thanks for telling them about us."

"Sure."

Seth's truck pulled to a stop out front, the headlights shining through the window.

"There's Seth," Taylor said.

She looked sad again. Emily wanted to hug her, but the girl didn't want that. "Remember—your mom is always with you," she said.

Without meeting her eyes, Taylor nodded, then turned and slipped out the door.

The girl's grief stayed with Emily, and throughout the next day, she thought about her often. She didn't get a chance to call Seth until late Friday afternoon. When he didn't answer, she left a message. "It's Emily. I'm calling about Taylor. When you have a minute, give me a buzz."

IN A BREAK during the poker game Friday night, Seth checked his cell phone for messages. Taylor might call, or some rancher with an emergency. To his relief, there was only one message—from Emily. Either a new dog had come in or one of the others was sick.

"Excuse me," he said, stepping into the hallway.

Frowning, he listened to the message. Why did she need to talk about Taylor? She'd seemed fine when he'd dropped her off at Cat's a few hours ago. It must not be too important or she'd have contacted him before now. And yet something was important enough that she'd called. Deep in thought, he returned to Tim Carpenter's living room.

"Everything okay?" Nick asked as Seth took his place at the card table.

"Emily left a message. She needs to talk to me about Taylor."

"You worried?" Sly asked.

"A little, but Taylor's at Cat's tonight." Seth pushed his concerns away. "I'll touch base with Emily tomorrow. I'm here to win back the money I've lost, and then take you three for more. Whose turn is it to deal?"

"Mine," Carpenter said. Roughly a decade older than Seth, he had a gruff manner, but seemed like a decent enough guy.

"Speaking of Emily," Sly said, while Carpenter shuffled the deck. "She's coming over next week to meet us and talk about a dog. The process seems almost as complicated as adopting a kid."

Sly ought to know—he and Lana had adopted their son.

"Emily doesn't let just anyone adopt a shelter dog. She makes sure she places them in good homes." Seth picked up his card. Pleased to see a pair of kings, he pushed two blue chips to the center of the table.

Carpenter tossed in two more. "I'll raise you."

"I wouldn't if I were you," Sly said.

The two men seemed tight. Seth envied Carpenter for that. He wished he knew how to get tight with his brother again.

For now at least, the tension between them had faded, overrun by the competitive nature of the game.

Around nine, the game broke up, as the other three poker players were ranchers and needed to be up early.

Seth had enjoyed himself as he hadn't in a long time. Joking and bluffing had taken his mind off Taylor, the slower than anticipated growth of his business, his shrinking savings and Emily. He'd eaten a ton of nuts, jerky and chips with dip, had smoked a cigar and drunk a couple beers. Best of all, he'd come out even, winning as much money as he'd lost.

He wasn't supposed to pick up Taylor until late tomorrow morning. Barring emergencies, he planned to sleep in, a luxury he rarely had time for.

He walked out with Nick and Sly, and then drove Sly back to Pettit Ranch. In the darkness, the thin coating of snow covering the fields glinted under his headlights. The highway was clear but slippery, and he drove with care.

"Any time you need a fourth, I'm available," he told Sly.

"I'll keep that in mind."

"Tim Carpenter's an interesting character."

"A bit rough around the edges, but not a bad guy." Sly yawned.

"Tired?" Seth asked as he pulled up Sly and Lana's driveway.

"Dead on my feet."

Seth pulled to a stop near the front porch. Sly opened his door and then glanced over his shoulder at him. "Good night, little brother."

He hadn't called Seth "little brother" since before Seth had left town. Hearing it felt good, and he grinned. "Night, Sly."

Traffic on the highway was light. It was still relatively early—plenty of time to head for a nearby bar and check out the women. But he wasn't in the mood. Besides, it had been a long week and he was tired. Ready to call it a night, he turned toward home.

Seconds later, he snorted. "Thirty-five years old, and too old for a wild night out—that's pitiful."

Surprising himself a few minutes later, he changed his mind about going home, and headed for Emily's instead.

Chapter Twelve

The lights were on in Emily's apartment, and Seth thought he heard Susannah barking up there. It took her a while to answer the front door.

"Seth." Twin lines formed between her brows. "What are you doing here?"

Why *was* he here? Seth rubbed the back of his neck. "I was passing by and figured this was a good time to talk about Taylor—if you let me in."

After hesitating, she opened the door wider and stepped back. Once inside, he noted her loose, faded sweatshirt, raggedy jeans and fuzzy slippers. Her hair was pulled into a knot on top of her head with a plastic clip, and loose strands floated around her face. She looked sexy—go figure.

"Uh, were you in bed?" he asked, imagining her there, naked under him.

"In these clothes?" She laughed. "I was cleaning my apartment."

"On a Friday night?"

"I know, I'm pathetic." The fine lines returned and deepened, and she crossed her arms. "I thought we made an agreement not to be alone together."

"Right, but you wanted to tell me about Taylor, and since I was out, I figured I may as well hear it in person." Her closed body language and slightly compressed lips let him know what she thought of that idea. He shouldn't have come. He reached for the door. "Never mind—I'll call you tomorrow instead."

"You drove all the way over here, and you're obviously

concerned about Taylor. You may as well stay. But I won't invite you upstairs, and let's keep our distance from each other."

"Agreed."

She sat down at Mrs. Oakes's desk. Seth took the couch across the room. "This far enough away?" he teased.

Her lips didn't so much as twitch.

"Where's Susannah?" he asked, crossing his foot over his knee.

"In the apartment." Emily pulled the clip from her hair and twisted it into a new knot. Not about to be corralled, the loose strands quickly fluttered free.

"I've never seen you with your hair up like that," he said.

"It's not exactly flattering."

"I think it's cute. You could almost pass for a high school kid."

"Which is exactly why I only wear it up when I'm cleaning house. I'm thirty years old, and I don't want to look like a teen."

No one could mistake her for that. She didn't have a lot of curves, but she was all woman.

She sniffed the air and wrinkled her nose. "You reek of cigar smoke and beer."

"You can smell me all the way over there?" Seth figured he must stink pretty bad. "I played poker with my brother tonight, but I only had one cigar and two beers over three hours. I'm totally sober. Do you have any breath mints?"

Emily rooted through Mrs. Oakes's desk, then tossed him a packet of Tic Tacs. "Speaking of your brother, his wife, Lana, contacted me the other day. They heard about The Wagging Tail from Taylor. I'm going out to their ranch next week, to talk with them about adopting a dog."

"Sly mentioned that earlier tonight. Nick played poker, too, and another guy, a cousin of Sly's wife who owns the ranch adjacent to theirs. Did you know that Dani's pregnant?" He wasn't sure why he needed to share all that with Emily—wasn't sure she cared.

"I hadn't heard about Dani. Please tell her congratulations from me. So you played poker tonight. Did you win anything?"

"Yeah, but I lost some, too. In the end I came out even."

"Better than losing your shirt." Emily checked her watch. "It's barely nine-thirty. If the game broke up this early, it must've been a bore."

"Not at all." Seth shrugged. "You know how ranchers are—up at the crack of dawn. I actually enjoyed myself."

"You sound surprised about that."

"I was. Sly and I used to be close, but now things are a little tense," he admitted, wondering why he was also telling her about this. He didn't talk about his issues with his brother, not even with Dani. But now that he was here, he couldn't seem to keep his mouth shut.

Emily nodded. "The night when the shepherd had his epileptic fit, you mentioned something about a 'rocky road' with your family, but you never said what happened."

"Here's the nutshell version—I acted like a class-A jackass."

"We've all done things we're sorry about." She hugged her waist. "Like me, expecting Harvey to take me with him when he moved across the country."

"I'm thinking he's also a jackass."

"True." She flirted with a smile. "I realize now how lucky I was that I didn't go with him. Prosperity is my home, and leaving it and The Wagging Tail would have broken my heart. What makes you a 'class-A jackass'?"

She looked genuinely interested, and tonight Seth didn't need much coaxing.

"I told you that Sly and I lived with an uncle after our parents died, and that Uncle George didn't like kids," he said. "He pretty much left us alone—except when we irritated him. We did that way too often. Then, let's just say, things got ugly." Seth wasn't about to get into the nasty details of verbal smack downs and physical abuse. "We learned to steer clear of him. I was mad at the world. I got into fights, earned bad grades, skipped school, had a few scrapes with the law—stuff like that."

Remembering, he winced. "Someone needed to take me in hand, and my big brother got stuck with the job. Just before Sly finished high school, our uncle died. As soon as Sly graduated and I finished eighth grade, we packed up and moved back to Prosperity. He had this idea that we'd reunite with Dani and be a family again."

"And it happened," Emily said.

"Not exactly. We were gone four years. By the time we returned, Big Mama had become Dani's family. Sure, we saw a lot of her, but we never lived under the same roof again. Sly rented an apartment for him and me, and enrolled me in high school. He tried to parent me and tell me what to do. That worked real well." Seth snickered. "I got tired of being stuck under his thumb and tired of battling him all the time, so I quit school and hopped a bus out of town. I left a note for Sly and Dani so they wouldn't worry, and when I decided to settle in California a few months later, I sent a postcard. I didn't give them any contact information, just said I was okay."

Emily didn't comment, but she was easy to read. She thought that leaving Sly and Dani in the dark all those years had been mean and thoughtless. She was right.

Seth had also missed huge landmarks—his brother's wedding and the birth of his and Lana's daughter, as well as Dani's wedding and so much more. Now he felt like an outsider, just punishment for his sins. He managed a sardonic smile. "Told you I was a jackass."

"You were young and impulsive, and hurting," she said with sympathetic look. "At least you let them know you were okay. Believe me, that's a big deal. When my father took off, he never contacted us again."

Emily had suffered through her own piece of hell, Seth realized. "That had to hurt. How old were you?"

"Nine."

The same age Taylor had been when Annabelle had asked Seth to move out, and probably one reason she and Emily got along so well.

"It's good that you decided to move back here when you took custody of Taylor," Emily said.

Seth agreed. "A dying friend who was also estranged from his family told me I'd best come home and make up with mine while I still could. Then when I found out about Taylor...I figured that now was the right time." He wanted badly to make amends. "I won't lie—I also wanted to show them that even though I'd dropped out of high school way back when, I managed to earn my GED, and graduate college and grad school. That I made something of myself."

His success was the one thing he felt good about and proud of.

"A week or so before the move, I contacted Sly and Dani and let them know I was coming home, and explained about Taylor. That's when I found out just how pissed off at me they were." He was still shaking his head at himself and what a thoughtless jerk he'd been. "Turns out that the whole seventeen years I was gone, they'd been trying to find me. If that doesn't make me a class-A jackass, I don't know what does."

Emily looked pensive. "Well, it's all behind you now. Still, I understand where they're coming from. You don't have a big family to begin with. It's the same with my mom, stepdad and me. We don't always see eye to eye. Heck, a lot of the time, they drive me crazy." She smiled at that. "But we're still family. You, Sly and Dani are *family*, and I'm sure they're happy that you're here now."

Maybe Dani was, but not Sly. Sure, he was probably relieved that Seth was alive and well, but that was as far as it went.

Seth stifled a frustrated groan. Sometimes he wished he could go back and redo the parts of his life that he'd botched up, but that was impossible. "Have you had any contact with your father?" he asked.

Emily looked sad. "About six years ago I hired a private investigator to track him down. It turned out he'd developed a drug problem and had lived on the streets for years. He died when I was in high school."

"That's terrible," Seth said.

"Yeah." She sighed. "At least my mom and I know what happened to him. Back to Dani. That time at the bowling alley, she didn't seem at all angry with you."

"She's a lot more forgiving than Sly. It's not so easy to get back into his good graces."

"Have you tried apologizing?"

"Not in so many words, but he knows I have regrets."

"Are you sure? He can't read your mind. You really should apologize."

"We're guys. We don't talk about those kinds of things."

Until now, Seth had never shared his personal stuff with anyone. He didn't know why he'd chosen Emily. Now that he'd aired his story, he was tired of talking about his sorry self. "I came here to find out about Taylor. I thought she was doing okay. Then your call came in. What's she done?" he asked warily.

"She's been doing well, but the other day, when we were outside enjoying her first snow, she made a few comments I think you should hear about."

Emily's sober expression worried him. Not at all sure he was ready, he mentally braced himself. "Such as?"

"This is between us, okay? She didn't swear me to secrecy or anything, but she probably wouldn't want me telling you."

"It stays between us—you have my word."

Emily looked relieved. "We were talking about how no two snowflakes are alike, and she was testing the theory by studying what landed on her coat sleeve. One in particular reminded her of a necklace she'd given her mother. She had the undertaker place it around her neck so that she was buried with it.

"She actually cried, Seth, but I could tell she didn't want me to see." Emily's eyes welled up, no doubt in sympathy. "She acts tough, but she really misses her mom."

He could identify. His own mother had died when he was just a kid, his father following her a year later. "I don't doubt that," he said, wishing he could ease the pain. "This whole adjustment has been really tough on her. Thanks for sharing this."

"There's more." Emily squared her shoulders, as if fortifying herself to reveal a weighty truth. "She claims that you walked out on her and her mother."

Seth couldn't have been more stunned if she'd slugged him in the chest. "What?"

"Apparently that's what her mother told her."

He did a slow burn and muttered a few choice four-letter words. "Is there anything else?"

"I'm afraid so." Emily bit her lip. "Taylor believes you left because you didn't want her in your life."

"That's a total lie," he said through gritted teeth.

He scrubbed his hand over his face. Then, too rattled to sit, he stood and began to pace the room. "Annabelle left me without a thought for Taylor. If she was still alive, I swear, I'd wring her neck. She took Taylor away, where I couldn't find her."

"Hold on there—you're jumping to conclusions," Emily said. "Annabelle may have told Taylor that *you* left *them,* but I asked Taylor if her mother had actually said you didn't want her. She answered no, but said that it was obvious."

"Because I didn't get in touch with her. Believe me, I tried, but I couldn't find her." Remembering that helpless anger, he paced to the wall, turned and paced back. The feeling had been similar to when his parents had died and the courts had separated him and Sly from Dani, and sent them to Iowa.

Pace, pace, turn. With sudden insight he realized that his anguish over losing contact with Taylor wasn't unlike the pain Dani and Sly had suffered over his disappearance.

He was worse than a class-A jackass. *Pace, pace, turn.* He was a stupid bastard. And shaken to the core.

A couple times as a kid, when he'd displayed the slightest vulnerability toward anything, whether a girl or an animal, good old Uncle George had punched him one to make him stronger.

Those punches had only made him angry, and he'd learned to wall off his feelings. Which pretty much explained his inability to open up and love anyone. Tonight, though, emotions flooded out of him like water through a broken dam. "What the hell am I supposed to do now?" he muttered.

"First, stop pacing—you're making me jumpy," Emily said. "Second, explain what happened to Taylor. Tell her the truth."

Nowhere near ready to sit again, Seth glared at Emily and kept moving. "According to you, talking cures everything."

His tone was as harsh as his expression, but she didn't so much as flinch. "Because it's the best way I can think of to work out a problem," she told him calmly. "At least, most of the time. Okay, it didn't work so well with my ex, mainly because he'd fallen out of love with me. If he ever loved me in the first place."

She let out a self-conscious laugh. "In hindsight, I have my doubts. I know that no one can talk another person into loving them. But with you…I'm pretty sure Taylor has deep feelings for you, and you certainly care about her. If I were standing in your shoes, I'd talk things through with her. It can't hurt."

"Now I know why she hates me—she thinks I don't want her."

Seth felt sick to his stomach. And scared, too. He returned to the couch and sank down heavily. How was he supposed to fix this? Hell, he couldn't even fix the mess he'd caused between him and Sly.

He thought back to the countless relationships he'd ruined in his life. God, he was a screwed-up mess.

"You're upset," Emily said softly.

His laugh sounded more like a howl of pain. "Damn straight I am."

Unable to meet her eyes, he rested his forehead in his hands. But he heard her stand and walk around the desk.

WITH HIS HEAD in his hands and his massive shoulders hunched, Seth looked defeated. Tension and hurt radiated from him in waves so thick that Emily could almost see them.

Her heart ached for him, and she forgot about keeping her distance. Wanting, needing to ease his pain, she sat down beside him on the couch. He didn't acknowledge her.

She nudged him with her elbow. "You're way too keyed up. Turn your back to me."

Now he looked at her, a dark frown on his face. "What for?"

"So that I can work some of that tension out of you."

He gazed at her with bleak eyes. "Why would you do that?"

"Because you're a good man."

Muttering something that sounded like, "The hell I am," he turned away from her and bowed his head to bare his neck.

Kneeling to reach him more easily, Emily started with his shoulders. His muscles were knotted and rock hard. His neck was just as bad.

While she kneaded out the kinks, her mind whirled.

He'd been through so much, and so had his siblings. And poor Taylor, thinking he didn't want anything to do with her, when he'd been every bit as torn up as her by their separation.

Seth let out a satisfied moan. "God, that feels good."

"I'm glad it's working. Your shoulders and neck are much looser now. If you lean forward, I'll do lower."

He bent at the waist, exposing his long, broad back. His shirt rode up a fraction, revealing a small wedge of male skin. Not an ounce of extra fat on him anywhere—just muscle. Under her ministrations, the tension in his corded biceps slackened and eased.

Not long ago, these powerful arms had held her. Tonight she hungered to feel them around her again. She hungered for more than that, for things she shouldn't want.

It wasn't too late to move away and ask him to leave. That would be the smart thing to do, but at the moment, Emily didn't care about smart.

A low sound of desire filled the air. From her own lips, she realized.

Seth sat up, his head snapping her way. His silvery, hot eyes speared her. "Emily," he said, his voice hoarse. "You're killing me."

She swallowed. "I am?"

"Uh-huh." His warm hands cupped her face. "For the love of all the animals on the planet, if I don't kiss you, there's no telling what will happen."

Her breath hitched and her breasts began to tingle. "I feel the same way. But my dogs and I need you here at The Wagging Tail, and I don't want to do anything that might cause you to leave before the end of the semester." She needed the time to find a replacement. Unless… "Um, but if you decide to stay on longer…we could really use your services."

He didn't even pause to think that over, just shook his head. "I gave you my word that I'll stay until Taylor's community service ends. That's all the time I can spare. Until then, I'm not going anywhere."

He swept his thumb across her bottom lip, his eyes silvery with heat. "You do understand that I have too much on my plate to get seriously involved."

"You know I feel the same way." She meant that. She did. At least she thought so. At the moment, it was hard to think *what* she wanted.

As long as Seth volunteered at the shelter at least until the end of the semester, and she kept her heart safe, which she definitely would, everything would be fine.

He tilted her chin up but didn't make a move, which was teasing but intoxicating. Humming with need, she puckered her lips in a silent plea.

He captured her mouth with so much need and passion that she forgot to think. His kisses quickly grew deeper and hungrier, making her long for more.

Then somehow she was on her back on the lumpy couch, with Seth bracing his weight above her. His eyes were closed. He had thick eyelashes, the kind she'd always wished she had. She ran her fingers over the planes of his face and felt the stubble of his beard.

His eyes opened, slits of molten silver. "What are you doing?"

"Exploring your face."

"I'd rather explore your body." He cupped her breast and groaned. "You're not wearing a bra."

Emily was so immersed in sensations and pleasure that she could barely form a reply. "I...I never wear one when I clean house."

His low chuckle rumbled through her. "From now on, whenever you get the urge to clean, call me. I'll come right over and help."

He pushed her sweatshirt all the way up and silently studied her.

Two of the things she disliked about her body were her

boyish hips and her small breasts. But Seth's groan of pure male satisfaction made her feel voluptuous and sexy. Her nipples tightened and she grew damp between her legs.

His expression was intent and sensuous as he skimmed one finger lightly across her nipples. Emily moaned and gave herself over to him.

Then, yes! His mouth replaced his finger. Later, when she was squirming with need, he unbuttoned her jeans, pulled the zipper down and slid his hand inside her panties. Between her legs, right where she wanted him.

Dear God in heaven.

She wished they were both naked, but Seth soon made her forget everything but the pleasure.

He knew just what to do, slipping his fingers inside her and moving his thumb across her most sensitive part. Delicious tension coiled low in her belly. Moments later, with a shudder, she climaxed.

He kissed her again, another deep, long kiss. After tugging her zipper closed, he sat up, pulling her with him, and straightened her sweatshirt.

"I'm leaving now, while I still can. Otherwise, I just might take you upstairs to bed and finish this."

As much as Emily wanted him, she shook her head. "I'm not ready for that."

"Didn't think so."

Filled with doubt, she walked him to the door. "You're sure that what just happened won't cause problems?"

He glanced at his erection and gave a wry smile. "Oh, there's a problem, all right, but nothing I haven't dealt with a million times before. Even so, I feel better than I did earlier."

"What are you going to do about Taylor?"

"I'm not sure, but when I figure it out, I'll let you know. Good night, Emily." He kissed her again, with a tenderness that left her aching for more.

Through a slit in the blinds, she watched him drive away.

Chapter Thirteen

"Did you and Cat enjoy yourselves?" Seth asked as Taylor buckled herself into the truck. On the drive to pick her up, he'd made up his mind to take Emily's suggestion and talk to her—after he gauged her mood.

"It was okay," Taylor said in the understated way he'd come to expect.

She wasn't wearing her usual tough-girl expression, and she didn't reach for her earbuds. Yep, she was in a decent enough mood for a talk.

"What'd you do?" he asked.

"Ate pizza, watched movies and stuff." She shrugged.

"What about Cat's parents?"

"After the pizza came, they left us alone." She yawned. "Her mom made waffles this morning."

"Sounds good."

Taylor yawned again.

"You're tired." He wasn't surprised. Sleepovers had nothing to do with sleep. "This is a good day for a nap."

"Yeah."

"How about some music," he said, gesturing at the radio. "You pick the station."

He didn't have to ask twice. She fiddled with the buttons until she found a Nirvana song. Not the country-and-western music Seth preferred, but he could live with it.

They lapsed into silence, and he decided to wait a little longer to talk to her.

It was a cold, gray, October afternoon, made for sitting

in front of the fire and watching football. Or burrowing under the covers with a willing woman.

With Emily.

As responsive as she'd been last night, he could imagine what sex with her would be like. His body began to stir. He willed it to behave.

It was a relief that she didn't want to get serious any more than he did. He wasn't going to think about the other part of the evening. Baring his soul to her when he would have been better off keeping his big mouth shut.

Now she'd seen him at his worst, his weakness exposed.

Since those bad years with Uncle George, Seth never let anyone see him as Emily had last night. But the things she'd shared about Taylor had hit him where it hurt, and he'd been too stunned to play tough.

He'd half expected her to mock him for revealing his pain. Instead, she'd worked the kinks out of his tense muscles. Her warmth and concern had turned him on even more than before.

Seth wasn't sure what that meant, and didn't want to know.

He was almost home now. Time for that talk while Taylor was a captive audience.

"I had a good time at the poker game," he said, wading in cautiously.

She gave him a sideways look. "Did you win any money?"

"You sound just like Emily." He chuckled. "I came out even, which is better than losing."

"You talked to Emily last night?" Taylor looked curious.

"I saw her."

Her eyes narrowed a fraction. "Are you dating her?"

What the hell had given her that idea? "Nah—we're friends." Although technically, after last night they were a lot more than that. "She called during the poker game, and after I dropped off Sly, I stopped by. She's going over to his and Lana's next week to interview them about adopting a dog, and is real happy you recommended The Wagging Tail."

Taylor looked pleased before her expression turned apathetic. "They know that you and I both volunteer at the shelter."

"Yeah, but I never thought to suggest they adopt a dog from there. You did." Curious, he turned the conversation back to Emily. "Emily and I aren't dating, but if we were, I get the feeling you wouldn't like it."

"What difference would that make? You'll just do what you want. My mom always did."

Interesting. "How so?"

A shrug. "Most of the guys she dated were total losers. I tried to tell her, but she didn't listen."

She hadn't had an easy time, and Seth imagined that Annabelle hadn't, either. "Some people are hard learners," he said. "They only learn through experience. In that way, your mom and I were alike. But I promise that the one thing I will always do is listen to you."

And it was time to get down to the nitty-gritty. He weighed his words carefully. After braking for a red light, he met her eyes. "I hope you don't put me in the same loser category as some of your mom's exes."

Taylor was silent, her expression blank. She could have been thinking anything.

"Look, I know these past few months haven't been easy for you," he said as the light turned green and he drove on. "You've had huge changes to adapt to—losing your mom unexpectedly, coming to live with me, leaving San Diego and moving to Prosperity. None of that is easy, and there aren't many people who could adjust. But you're handling it like a trouper, and I'm real proud of you. And, Taylor…" He had to stop and clear his throat. "I'm sorry your mom is gone, but I'm awful glad you're back in my life."

She blinked in surprise, and he caught a glimpse of the

vulnerable girl she was, before her expression hardened. He barely had time to wonder at that before she spoke.

"You never told me about the house."

It took him a minute to figure out that she meant their rental. Weeks had passed since Emily had mentioned his plan to Taylor, and the subject had never come up. "That's right," he said. "I want to buy it and fix it up for the two of us. I didn't think you were interested in hearing about that."

"I'm not." She rummaged through her tiny purse. Moments later she slid out her iPod and earbuds, put them on and turned her face toward the passenger window. Shutting him out once again.

That had gone real well. Seth winced.

He wasn't sure what kind of reaction he'd expected, but not this. He swore softly. Emily was wrong—talking with Taylor had been a bust.

He wished he had a plan B to fall back on, but for the life of him, he couldn't think what it should be.

IN THE KENNEL, Emily stood across the exam table from Seth and held firmly on to one of the shelter's newer arrivals, a medium-size male who looked to be part retriever, part Welsh corgi. Seth had cleared him from quarantine days ago, but the poor pooch had something in his paw. Scared and in pain, he shook and whimpered.

It was a relief that her Wednesday morning volunteers had taken the other dogs out. They'd probably be upset by this.

"That hurts, huh?" Seth murmured to the animal, in the steady, calming tone Emily had come to expect.

Although his big, capable hands dwarfed the tweezers, he wielded them with practiced skill. Since their passionate make-out session Saturday night Seth and his hands had filled almost her every waking thought. And his mouth… Emily stifled a dreamy sigh.

Oh, she wanted him.

But what really melted her was that he'd opened up and shared his past and his fears about Taylor. That couldn't have been easy for him. She so liked this man, and every time she was with him, no matter how hard she fought herself, her feelings grew. If she wasn't careful, she'd wind up with a broken heart.

No, thank you.

She wasn't going to let that happen, wouldn't let herself fall in love. Not now, and not with Seth. He didn't want love, and neither did she.

Got that, heart?

She really should keep her distance from him, but this morning, he needed her help while he worked. Although if she were honest, she'd admit that he could probably handle the dog by himself. Yet here she was.

He extracted a long thorn from the dog's right front paw and held it up for her to see. "Look at the size of this thing."

Emily was appalled. "No wonder he's been limping and crying. I wonder where he picked that up."

"Beats me, but the paw's infected. He needs antibiotics. I'll phone in a prescription. Meanwhile, I happen to have some ointment with me that will ease the pain and soothe the inflammation."

After applying the salve, he gently wrapped the injured paw. "Leave this bandage on for as long as you can."

Emily nodded.

"Good boy," he told the dog, gently ruffling the fur between his ears. Seth set him back in his cage, then washed up. Emily shrugged into her parka and walked out with him.

From out of nowhere, an icy wind blew through the yard. Despite her heavy jacket, she shivered. By the calendar, they weren't quite a month into autumn, yet it felt like winter.

"I was really impressed with your brother and his wife when I visited Pettit Ranch on Monday," she said as they headed toward Seth's pickup. "They're coming here today, and should arrive soon."

"They have a nice spread. Which dog do you think they'll want?"

Emily thought about that. In the six weeks since Seth had first volunteered, all the dozen and a half or so animals he'd treated had been adopted. Now, counting the male he'd just seen, there were six more available, some more suitable than others for a family with young children.

"The bulldog-poodle and spaniel-terrier mixes are the gentlest," she said. "I don't think either of them has been abused, so they should be able to tolerate kids."

Seth nodded. He hadn't mentioned Taylor since the other night. Curious, Emily broached the subject. "Have you and Taylor had a chance to talk?"

A pained look crossed his face. "I tried."

"Things didn't go well?"

"Nope. I didn't get very far before she shut me out. That was Saturday, and she's barely said two words to me since." He scrubbed his hand over his face. "Told you I suck at talking about personal stuff."

Emily felt for him. "Maybe it'll go better next time."

He gave her an *are you crazy?* frown and stopped in his tracks. "Suffer through this crap again? I'll pass."

He couldn't just leave things the way they were. It wasn't good for either him or Taylor. "I know it's hard, Seth, but you can't give up," Emily said. "You two *have* to talk, and sooner is better than later."

"Easy for you to say. You don't have to live with her."

"But I—" The sudden set of his jaw and his slightly narrowed eyes silenced her.

"You're not a therapist, and Taylor isn't your problem. So butt out."

Apparently she'd hit a sore spot. And here she'd thought Seth had trusted her enough to discuss the situation. Emily was taken aback and a little intimidated. But she'd never been one to hold in her opinion, especially when she was fighting for something that mattered. And Seth's relationship with Taylor mattered a great deal.

"You two are both hardheaded," she said. "You need help. *Someone* has to get involved, and it may as well be me."

EMILY FACED SETH with her hands on her hips and her chin up. He'd just told her to butt out, and had fixed her with the stern look that shut most people up.

But not her.

He wasn't used to that and wasn't sure what to make of her. Yet, he knew one thing for certain—the way she'd stood up to him was sexy. But then, everything about her turned him on.

The cold wind ruffled her hair. She pushed it back, out of her eyes. His unwitting gaze flitted over her. He'd never seen a hot-pink parka before. Pink wasn't his thing, but it sure looked good on her. He also liked the snug-fitting jeans and her long legs.

He liked Emily, period. And despite her unwanted advice, he wanted her more than ever. But dammit, she teed him off. "You don't quit, do you?" he muttered.

"Not when—"

Tired of her unwanted advice, Seth kissed her.

A long, thorough kiss that had her melting against him. His mind blanked. He was unzipping her parka when the sound of a car penetrated his clouded mind.

Sly and Lana's burgundy minivan rolled up the driveway. Damn. Seth stepped back.

Looking dazed, Emily tugged her parka down and smoothed her hair.

By the smiles on his brother and sister-in-law's faces, they'd seen everything.

Seth swore under his breath. Should've kept his hands to himself. But around Emily, that was impossible.

"What are you doing here?" Sly's mouth quirked. "Besides making out with Emily."

Seth scowled at him. "I was treating a sick dog."

"Is that what you call it?"

Seth had had enough. "I have an appointment—gotta go." That was true. For the first time since he'd hung out his shingle in Prosperity, he had three appointments scheduled in one afternoon. If business kept picking up, he'd soon be able to add to his savings and build up what he needed to buy the house. "Good luck choosing a dog."

Out of her car seat, Johanna raced toward him. "Hi, Unca Seth! Hi, Emily!"

Squealing, Mark toddled behind her.

Seth greeted his niece and nephew and bid his goodbyes. Then he tossed his medical bag into the pickup, climbed in and took off.

Chapter Fourteen

"That's two businesses we signed up so far!" Taylor exclaimed after she and Cat exited a hardware store.

They were spending today's community-service hours in downtown Prosperity, soliciting donations for The Wagging Tail's silent auction. She'd never imagined that signing people up would be this easy.

She and Cat high-fived. When they hung out together, Taylor didn't think about her mom, and forgot that Seth had taken her in only because he was forced to. She didn't miss San Diego so much, either. Even if it was cold here.

Her feet were freezing, and despite her gloves, so were her hands. "We deserve a break, someplace where we can get warm," she said.

Cat didn't reply. She was too busy watching a boy and girl across the street share a kiss, right there on the sidewalk. A moment later, they broke apart and smiled at each other. Holding hands, they turned the corner.

Cat sighed. "That's how I'd like to get warm. I wish I had a boyfriend."

Taylor wouldn't have minded, either. Although boys didn't seem interested in her. Anyway, Seth probably wouldn't let her date. He thought she was a baby, which was even worse than her mom. She'd set Taylor's curfew at eleven o'clock—one of the many things they'd fought about. Seth was even worse. He expected her to call when she got home from school, as if she was a little kid. "Where to next?" she said.

"How about—" Cat cut herself off and nodded at a lanky boy striding up the next block. "He's cute."

"*Really* cute," Taylor agreed. "Is he going into Java Jim's? We can warm up there *and* ask the manager to donate to the fund-raiser."

"What are we waiting for?" Cat asked.

A few minutes later, giggling and smoothing their hair, they pushed the heavy glass door open and entered Java Jim's.

The boy already had a drink and was taking it to a booth. As they passed him on their way to the order counter, he smiled.

"Up close, he's even cuter," Cat murmured under her breath.

The manager wasn't in, so they left their phone numbers with the girl who took their coffee orders. They bought cookies, too. In no time, they were carrying mugs and treats to a booth across from the boy's.

He was doing something on his phone, but as soon as they sat down, he set it aside and grinned. "Hey."

Cat smiled back. "Hey."

"Hi." Taylor flashed her own smile, but his attention was on Cat.

"I haven't seen you in here before," he said.

"This is our first time."

They talked back and forth, Taylor, too, exchanging their names. Isaac was sixteen and attended Denton High. He had an after-school job at Java Jim's. This was his day off, but he liked hanging out here. He was doing his community service at the local YMCA. Taylor and Cat told him about The Wagging Tail and the silent auction.

"I'll put in a good word with Derek, the manager, " Isaac promised.

"That'd be great," Taylor said.

"Hey, do you want to sit with us?" Cat asked.

"Yeah." Isaac slid in beside her, across from Taylor.

At first, he conversed with them both, but before long he was talking only to Cat. Taylor finished her coffee and cookie. She pulled out her phone and texted Hanna and Kayla, her two best friends in San Diego. She'd been out of touch with them for days. Both texted back, but they were busy and had to go.

Cat and Isaac were talking about music now, neither of them even glancing at Taylor. Sitting there with nothing to do was boring and uncomfortable. "Excuse me," Taylor said, scooting out of the booth to use the bathroom.

Neither seemed to notice. Feeling invisible, just as she had when her mom had had a boyfriend, she followed the sign for the restrooms. During those times, her mom had tended to forget Taylor existed. Seth had been the one boyfriend of her mom's who'd paid attention to Taylor and treated her like she mattered.

But it turned out that he hadn't really cared, either.

As she headed back to the booth, she wished she was at home—no, Seth's house wasn't home, she reminded herself. She was only there temporarily. Still, she wished she was at the house now, in her room, listening to music and doing whatever. At least then she wouldn't feel like she'd been forgotten.

Instead of sitting down, she checked the time. "It's getting late," she said. "We need to catch a bus back to the shelter."

"I guess I have to go." Cat tore her gaze away from Isaac.

"Can I have your phone number?" he asked.

"If you give me yours."

They traded phones and input the information.

As Cat stood, Isaac followed suit. "Are you busy tomorrow night?"

She gave him a big smile. "As a matter of fact, I'm not."

On the way to the bus stop, she made a *squee* sound and pirouetted. "I have a date with Isaac!"

As the bus headed toward the shelter, she talked nonstop

about how much she liked him. She didn't say one word about leaving Taylor out of the conversation.

Taylor was happy for her friend, but also a little jealous. Did Cat even care if she was around?

SATURDAY AFTERNOON, Emily headed for Pettit Ranch to gauge how the Pettit family and the spaniel-terrier female they'd adopted were adjusting to each other. A phone call would probably suffice, but she preferred to see for herself. After the visit, she'd go home and tackle a few of the must-finish items on her fund-raiser to-do list. Not exactly a thrilling way to spend a Saturday evening, but with the event just three weeks away, getting things done was a priority.

Lana let her into the beautiful Pettit home with a smile on her face and a wiggly toddler in her arms. "Hi, Emily. Come in."

"Thanks. Hi, Mark."

"Hi," the little boy managed to say before his mother put him down.

"Be gentle and don't scare the doggie, okay?" Lana told him. He moved silently into the great room.

"She gets skittish when there's too much noise," Lana explained as she hung up Emily's coat.

It had been only three days. "Give her time and she'll adjust."

In the great room, dog and kid toys lay scattered across the carpet. Sly was sprawled on the floor, Mark now in his lap. Beside them, Johanna "read" a book. The picture of domestic tranquility.

Emily envied the family. Sly and Lana had what she eventually wanted—a great marriage and cute kids. *Someday,* she told herself. When she was ready and met the right man.

The spaniel-terrier's sleeping cage sat against the wall. The door was open and the dog inside, where she probably felt safer. Although her ears pricked forward in clear interest and curiosity, she stayed put.

"Hey, Emily," Sly called softly. "The pooch is doing okay. I'll see if I can coax her out."

He offered her a dog biscuit, his gentleness reminding Emily of Seth. The Pettit brothers were both big, handsome men, with the same silver-blue eyes, but Seth was the one who made her go weak.

The offer of a treat was too good to resist, and the dog ventured out. Already she'd put on some weight, a good sign.

As soon as she gobbled down her biscuit, Johanna and Mark clapped—noise that sent her dashing back into the cage.

Johanna looked stricken. "We scared her."

"Scared," Lana corrected, ruffling her daughter's hair. "She's a little shy, just like your brother is around strangers."

"That's right." Emily nodded. "She'll get used to you."

"She'd better," Sly muttered. He didn't look happy.

"Are you having second thoughts about keeping her?" Emily asked, hoping that he wasn't. The dog deserved the chance at a normal life with these wonderful people.

Lana gaped at her. "No way. She's a member of our family now."

Emily let out a relieved breath.

"Tell Emily what you named her," Lana said to her daughter.

"Brown Cow, 'cause she's brown and white, just like a root-beer float." Johanna licked her lips. "My favoritest drink in the whole world."

Emily laughed. "That's a perfect name for her."

Lana smiled. "We shortened it to Brownie."

"Bohnie," Mark crowed.

Having seen all that she needed in order to reassure herself, Emily thanked the family and turned to leave.

"It's almost dinnertime," Lana said. "Why don't you stay? We have plenty of food—if you don't mind meat loaf."

Despite the pile of work waiting at home, Emily was strongly tempted. She didn't have to stay late, and it *would* be nice to eat with the Pettit family. "I love meat loaf, and I'd like to join you," she said. "But only if you let me help with the meal."

"Of course." Lana checked her watch. "We should probably get started—Seth and Taylor should be here any minute."

"They're coming to dinner?" Emily asked, trying to appear nonchalant.

Lana nodded. "Is that a problem?"

Only because Emily liked Seth so much. "Of course not—if you don't think they'll mind that I'm here."

"The way Taylor sings your praises whenever we see her?" Lana shook her head. "She'll be thrilled."

"I know Seth won't mind, either." Sly's lips quirked.

No doubt he was thinking about the kiss he'd caught them sharing. Telltale warmth climbed Emily's face, and she knew she was blushing.

Lana hooked arms with her. "We'll be in the kitchen. Johanna and Mark, you and Daddy keep Brownie company."

After Emily washed up, Lana handed her a knife and an apron, directed her to slice potatoes, and began to gather ingredients for the meat loaf.

"Don't say anything about that kiss, okay?" Emily cautioned. "Taylor has no idea."

"Your secret is safe with Sly and me. I don't think the kids saw anything."

Emily barely released a relieved breath before Lana hit her with a question.

"What exactly is going on between you two?"

Wasn't that the billion-dollar puzzler. "I know what it looks like," Emily said. "But it's nothing—not really."

If you didn't count the hunger and passion that seemed to grow each time they were together.

Lana glanced up from the giant bowl where her hands were buried. "Do you want there to be?"

In her heart, Emily did, but her logical mind kept reminding her that getting serious was too risky. "My ex-fiancé and I broke up a year and a half ago," she explained. "I'm not ready for a new relationship."

"You're not over him yet."

"Oh, I definitely am. It's just…I'm a little wary of getting involved again."

"That makes sense. But maybe it's time to take a chance and see what happens."

Every time Emily talked to Bridget and Monica, which was at least once a week, they said the same thing. "I don't know." She glanced at the pile of sliced potatoes. "This isn't a good time for either Seth or me. Between the shelter and my web business, I'm super busy. He's just as busy juggling the building of his practice with the demands of a teenage girl."

"In other words, you're perfect for each other." Lana's smile was pure Cheshire cat.

Emily frowned. "How so?"

"You both love animals with a passion, you both care about Taylor and you kissed each other the other day like you meant it. In my book, that's a winning combination."

"Look, that's Emily's car," Taylor said as Seth pulled up at his brother's house just before dinnertime on Saturday. She sounded more animated than she had all day. "I wonder what she's doing here?"

So did Seth. "Sly and Lana took that dog home Wednesday, and Emily likes to follow up a few days later. She's probably checking to see how they're doing."

"Cool." Taylor was already out of the pickup.

By the time Seth reached the front door with a bouquet of flowers for the hostess, Taylor had disappeared inside.

He found her sitting on the floor in the great room, along with Emily, Sly and the kids. Nearby, the sleep cage of the dog they'd chosen from the shelter yawned open, with the dog inside sticking her nose out. Johanna was sitting close beside Taylor, and Mark had climbed onto her lap. Taylor was talking animatedly with Emily.

Her arms around her knees, Emily looked right at home. Suddenly, she laughed at something.

With her head back and laughter on her face, she was beautiful. Seth wanted her more than ever. As if she felt him watching her, she glanced up. Their gazes held, and his body jumped to life. Seth willed it to behave.

"You're here to check on the dog," he guessed.

She nodded. "She's doing great. Sly and Lana invited me to stay for dinner."

"Sweet," Taylor said.

Seth suspected the invitation had something to do with the kiss his brother and sister-in-law had witnessed the other day.

"Look at the gorgeous flowers Seth brought," Lana said, holding up the bouquet. "Wasn't that sweet?"

Seth's face got all hot, and his brother gave him a searching look. "I need a beer and you need a vase. Join me?"

In the kitchen, Sly rooted through a cabinet. He found a vase and handed it to Seth. "Make yourself useful. Want a beer?"

"Sure."

"That kiss I saw looked pretty hot," Sly commented as he pulled two cold ones from the fridge. "What's with you and Emily?"

His brother always had been blunt. Seth narrowed his eyes. "If you're trying to play matchmaker, quit. I like her, but we're not dating."

Although they sure were fooling around together.

"Why the hell not?" Sly asked.

"I'll give you two big reasons—Taylor and my practice."

Sly snorted. "You can't work all the time. As for Taylor, she worships the ground Emily walks on. She'd probably be happy if you and Emily started going out."

"I doubt that," Seth said. "She doesn't like me much. I wouldn't want any of that hostility to rub off on Emily."

"I don't see that happening. Give Taylor time and she'll come around—just like we're doing with Brownie."

If only it was that simple. "Brownie, huh?"

"Johanna picked out the name." Sly dug a bottle opener from a drawer and handed it to Seth.

They opened their beers. Instead of heading back to the great room, they settled on chairs at the breakfast bar.

Sly raised his bottle. "To adjusting to change."

They clinked bottles and drank. Since the poker game, the tension between them had lessened, and tonight Seth was more relaxed around his brother than he'd been in a long while.

It felt like the right time to apologize. Seth set down his beer. "Sly, I—" His throat clogged up, and he had to stop and swallow. "I shouldn't have stayed out of touch all those years. It was a crappy thing to do."

Sly didn't argue. "Damn straight. Put yourself in my place. Bad enough that you quit school and scribbled a one-sentence note when you took off. Months later we get one puny postcard, with zero contact information on it?" He gave a meaningful frown, took a sip of beer and went on.

"All those years, Dani and I wondered if you were dead or alive. Which sucked, and pretty much turned me off of having a family." He shook his head. "If Lana hadn't accidentally gotten pregnant, I don't know that I'd ever have married or had kids."

Seth knew about the unplanned pregnancy, but he'd had no idea about the rest. "From what I've seen, you're a great dad," he said.

"I try. But I screwed up so bad with you that I couldn't see doing the same thing to another kid."

Sly thought he was responsible for Seth's behavior? Seth squinted at him. "You didn't screw up, Sly. You're only three years older than me. Hell, you did the best you could. And I didn't exactly make life easy. I screwed myself up."

"Losing our parents and going to live with Uncle George didn't help." Sly's face darkened. "Those were bad times for both of us."

They both stared straight ahead, each taking long pulls on their beer.

Seth darted a glance at his brother. "Making things right with you—that's one reason I moved back here. I'd like to put the past behind us."

Sly was quiet for so long, Seth wasn't sure he'd heard. Finally, he cocked his head. "I can do that." Once again he raised his beer. "To moving on."

"Moving on," Seth repeated.

When they set their empty bottles on the bar, Sly clapped a warm hand on Seth's shoulder. "It's good to have you back in the family."

"It's great to be here."

They returned to the great room. Emily wore a questioning look—almost as if she guessed that something important had happened between him and Sly. Seth gave a slight nod toward his brother and grinned. Emily's brilliant smile lit him up inside. Man, he felt good.

"Um, Seth?" Wearing a curious frown, Taylor glanced from him to Emily.

He hoped she didn't ask about them. He wouldn't know what to say. For sure not the truth—that he spent way too much time fantasizing about getting naked with Emily. "Yeah?" he said, wary.

"Cat just texted and invited me to another sleepover at her house tonight. Can I go?"

"You mean right now?"

She shook her head. "After dinner."

"It's her turn to come over to our house."

"I want to go over there. Please."

"As long as no one minds if we eat and run," he said, but his eyes were on Emily.

"Don't look at me," she said. "I'm an impromptu guest here."

"Not a problem with us," Lana said.

Seth nodded at Taylor. "Then okay, you can go. But next time, Cat stays at our house."

A rare smile bloomed on Taylor's face, and for a minute, she looked as if she wanted to throw her arms around him. Naturally, she didn't, but it felt like a giant step in the right direction. Tonight, life seemed bright with promise.

That got him thinking.

Talking with Sly had turned out well. Hell, if he could iron out the mess with his brother, maybe he ought to try again to talk with Taylor. Couldn't hurt.

He would do it while she was in her good mood and a captive audience—tonight, on the drive to Cat's.

Chapter Fifteen

By the time Taylor packed an overnight bag and Seth steered toward Cat's house, night had fallen. Traffic was light, and from what he could tell, Taylor's good mood was holding. He was searching his mind for the right way to talk about the things he needed to say, when she started fishing through her purse. No doubt searching for her earbuds and iPod.

Forget choosing the perfect words. If he didn't start the conversation now, it wouldn't happen. "Can you hold off on the music?" he asked. "I want to talk to you."

She all but winced, as if she expected harsh things to come out of his mouth. *Damn.* "Relax—I'm not going to yell at you," he said. "I, uh… This is important."

He had her attention now. Scant light from the dash cast her face in shadow, making it harder to read her expression. But the inquisitive flash in her eyes was plain enough.

Here goes. He cleared his throat. "Those years when you were out of my life—I really missed you."

He felt her surprise, which was followed by a skeptical snort. "If that's true, why didn't you get in touch?"

Surely she knew the answer. Then again, why would she? Hadn't Annabelle told her that he'd walked away? "Because I had no idea where you were," he replied. "When your mom and I split up, I had every intention of keeping in contact with you, and I told her so. She never mentioned leaving town. I found out when I stopped by with a Hard Rock Café Barbie a few days later. You'd been asking for it for weeks."

"Why would you buy me that? You didn't have the money, and it wasn't my birthday."

"No, but I knew you'd be upset that I'd moved out. I wanted you to know that no matter what happened between your mom and me, I still cared about you. But when I got to the house, it was empty. I had no idea where you and your mom had gone."

Taylor gave him a sideways look. "You left first. My mom was so upset we *had* to go someplace new."

"That's what she said?" Seth started to utter a four-letter word, but stopped himself. He wasn't about to go off like that in front of Taylor. Besides, getting mad wouldn't solve anything. Gripping the wheel, he reined in his anger. "Your mom broke up with me because she wanted to get married and I didn't. I wasn't ready."

"No, *you* broke up with *us*. She said you never wanted to see us again. You sure never called. Why are you lying, Seth?"

"Everything I'm telling you is God's honest truth," Seth said evenly. "I did try to call. I loved you like you were my own flesh and blood. Losing you hurt like h—really bad. That first week after you left, I must have called your mom a dozen times. She wouldn't pick up. Then she got a new number, unlisted."

He remembered that awful time—the hollow feeling in his chest, wondering what Taylor was thinking, and knowing she was hurting as much as he was. "I spent years trying to find you. My whole life was divided between going to school, working and looking for you."

He'd given up hanging out with his buddies, hadn't dated. There'd been no time for those things.

For all his honesty, he got a curled lip from Taylor.

"I don't believe you." Although the heat in the truck was cranked up and she wore her winter jacket, she wrapped her arms around her waist as if she was cold. "My mom wouldn't lie."

And yet, she had. Seth halted at a four-way stop and looked hard at Taylor before he drove on. "If your mom really believed that I never wanted to see you again, why did she name me as your guardian?"

"Because she was out of her mind? I don't know. But she wouldn't lie."

Realizing that he wasn't going to change the teen's mind, he blew out a frustrated breath. "Believe what you want." A moment later, calmer, he went on. "If I could go back in time, I'd make sure your mom and I worked out a way for me to keep in touch with you. But you and I both know that we can't go back and change the past. We only have now. Your mother is gone, and you and I are both here together. That's not going to change."

Taylor maintained a stony silence. She wasn't softening at all. As usual, his attempt at a heart-to-heart had failed—his cue to give up and cut out. This time, he didn't have that option, wouldn't take it if he did. Taylor was too important to him.

They were almost at Cat's house. Not much time left for talking. There was only one thing to do—go for broke.

Sucking in a breath, Seth headed into unfamiliar territory. "I care about you, Taylor. Your being here... It means a lot to me. I want us to be a family," he finished, his voice breaking with feeling.

Hating that he was losing control, he clamped his jaw.

Spilling his guts got him nowhere. No reaction at all. Damn, that stung. His spirits plummeting, he signaled and pulled into Cat's driveway.

Taylor grabbed her stuff. As she reached for the door handle, she turned back to him. "I'll think about it."

Before he could react, she slid out of her seat and shut the door behind her.

A lump lodged in Seth's throat. He watched her stride to the front door and disappear inside the brightly lit home, this willowy, awkward teenage girl who'd turned his life upside down. Mulling over what had just happened, he backed out.

She hadn't exactly gushed out the "I want us to be a family, too, Seth" response he'd wanted, but at least she hadn't shut him out.

It was a start, and he felt outrageously good.

His thoughts flashed to Emily and the dinner at Sly's tonight. She got along great with the family, and her relationship with Taylor kept growing stronger.

Opening up and talking *had* helped. Emily had been right all along. Her insight and smarts had paid off, big time. She'd want to know about this.

Seth found a place to pull off the road.

She answered right away. "Hi." She sounded surprised. "That was a nice dinner tonight."

"Yeah."

"You and Sly cleared the air, huh? That's so great."

"Sure is. Listen, I just dropped Taylor off at Cat's. I talked to her tonight, too. Can I come over and tell you about it?"

She hesitated a moment, and his elation slipped a notch. He figured he could tell her right now, over the phone, but he preferred to do it in person. He wasn't about to question why being with her now was so important. It just was. "You have plans," he guessed.

"Big ones—working on the fund-raiser."

Seth scoffed. "On a Saturday night?"

"The big event is only three weeks away."

"Why are you so stressed about it? I thought you and your volunteers had lined up all the silent auction donors you need."

"There's still quite a bit to do."

"Can't you ask Taylor and the other high school kids to help you out? I'll bet the adult volunteers I met at the brainstorming thing would be happy to lend a hand, too."

"Believe me, next week they'll all be pitching in."

"Then it's settled—no work tonight. I sure don't want to sit around at home. Let's go out." On a whim, he decided where. "Ever played pool?"

"Once. I'm about as bad at it as I am at bowling."

"I'll give you some pointers. See you in a few."

He disconnected. Whistling, he pulled back onto the road and sped toward Emily's.

EMILY BARELY HAD time to brush her teeth before Seth knocked at the front door.

"He's here," she told Susannah, slightly breathless. Whether from running around getting ready, or simply because Seth had arrived, she wasn't sure. She gave the dog a quick back scratch. "See you later."

Downstairs, she checked her hair before she let him in. As soon as Seth strode through the door, she could see that something was different, even since dinner tonight. He seemed lighter, almost carefree. Without the usual solemnity and worry etching his face, he looked years younger. And breath-catchingly handsome.

Oh, she liked this man.

Lana's words came back to her. *Maybe it's time to take a chance and see what happens.* As scary as the thought was, Emily had to admit that it appealed to her. She just wished she knew where Seth stood.

He helped her into her coat, and she had to know. "Is this a date?"

When he paused, she knew the question had thrown him off.

"You sound like Taylor," he said. "A couple of weeks ago, she asked if we were seeing each other. She didn't like the idea."

"Really." Emily frowned, wondering where the girl's question had come from. She'd seen the two of them together only a few times. "What did you tell her?"

"That we aren't."

"So this isn't a date." *Oops.* She felt foolish for even letting her thoughts go there. "Taylor will be pleased about that."

"Hold on there." Seth's eyebrows notched toward each other. "The thing with Taylor was weeks ago. That was then and this is now. Yeah, this is a date."

Emily's mind spun with the possibilities. Once again, doubts consumed her. Given her growing feelings for Seth, and the risks to her heart, should she even go out with him tonight? Probably not.

"Look, I know you don't have time to date right now," he said, clearly misinterpreting her hesitation. "Neither do I, but it's Saturday night, and Taylor's gone until tomorrow. I don't think she'd be all that upset anymore, and I sure as hell don't want to sit at home, catching up on paperwork or watching the boob tube. We both deserve a night out. Why shouldn't we spend it together?"

At least she knew where things stood—that her feelings for Seth went deeper than his for her. "You make some good points," she said.

Reminding herself to keep her heart safe, she headed with him into the brisk night air. "I'm really curious about your conversation with Taylor."

Seth seemed eager to share it. "It happened on the drive to Cat's."

He opened the passenger door of his pickup and Emily climbed up. "What did you talk about?" she asked, when they were both seated and buckled in.

"The past, now…a lot of stuff. Things didn't go so well at first." Seth started the truck and drove toward the road. "Especially when I explained that it was never my intention to leave her, and that her mom took her away without a word to me. She didn't believe me, but she still listened."

"That's a positive sign," Emily said.

"Definitely." He rolled his shoulders and then cleared

his throat. "I told her that I care about her and that I want us to be a family."

What it would feel like to hear those words directed at *her*, Emily couldn't even imagine. And why should she? Seth didn't have those kinds of feelings for her, and neither did she toward him. Or so she told herself. "Pouring out your heart like that can't have been easy for you, Seth."

"It was worth the effort. She said she'd think about the family thing." Despite the darkness, the grin on his face was easy to see.

No wonder he was in such good spirits. "Sounds as if you two hit a milestone."

"To quote Taylor, it feels epic."

His giddiness was infectious and Emily laughed. "First you straighten things out with Sly, then you make headway with Taylor. You're on a roll tonight."

"Taylor and I still have a long road to travel, but things are definitely moving in the right direction. Thanks to you."

"Me?" Emily had no idea what he meant.

"You pushed me to talk to Sly, and you pushed me to try again with Taylor."

"Yes, and you about bit my head off."

"There is that." He didn't look at all contrite. "But hey, I took your advice, and it worked. I'm in a good place right now, and I want to celebrate with you."

In other words, keep it light tonight. She could do that. "Then let's. I assume we're going to Clancy's?"

"You know the place?"

"Only because in high school, a date took me there once."

"So that was your one time playing pool. Was he your boyfriend?"

Emily shook her head. "It was our first and last date."

"Was it him or the game?"

"Actually, it was me. He asked me out again, but I wasn't interested."

"I'll bet he was sorry about that. I'm guessing a lot of guys wanted to date you."

"Not really." Even back then, she'd been wary of getting too close to any boy. In hindsight, she realized her reluctance had been fallout from her father's leaving as he had. "You, on the other hand, probably had dozens of girls after you."

"Not that many, but a few. Back then, I was a bad boy. Some girls go for that."

Seth gave a sexy, cocky grin, and Emily pictured him as a teenage heartthrob, with girls vying for his attention.

"Did you play pool with any of your dates?" she asked.

"There was one girlfriend with a table at her house. I used to go over there and play with her and her dad. When she and I split up, I found a pool table at the YMCA and kept at it."

"So you play regularly?"

"Not anymore. Before I left Prosperity all those years ago, Sly, Dani and I played at Clancy's a few times. Then when I was in college, I competed in minor tournaments. I needed the money."

"At last, the truth comes out," she teased. "You must be really good."

"I'm not bad," he said with a modest shrug.

"And to think that I'm out with a pool shark."

Seth chuckled, and Emily knew that keeping things light was going to be easy.

A few minutes later the neon Clancy's sign came into view. The parking lot was full, so Seth found a spot on a side road.

The main hall was packed and noisy, but they found a pool table in an adjoining room in the back. Here, there was room for only two tables. The other was taken by an older couple in matching "I heart Clancy's" T-shirts. They nodded a greeting and then returned to their game.

To the accompaniment of country-and-western music

pounding from the old-time jukebox, Seth helped Emily choose a cue, and selected one for himself.

"You want to go first?" he said in a loud voice after racking the balls.

She shook her head. "You go ahead."

Seth chalked his cue and began. He made the game look easy, gracefully shooting balls straight into various pockets. At the rate he was clearing the table, Emily doubted she'd get a turn this game. Not that she minded. She was content to watch him.

The way his big body canted at the waist. The play of his arm and chest muscles, stretching his flannel shirt taut across his broad shoulders. His faded jeans and long legs, splayed and braced when he took a shot. And his very fine masculine butt. Everything about him was sexy, even his slightly scuffed boots.

He was also smart and warm. And great at kissing—and other things. Emily sighed. She could fall for him so easily.

That spooked her a little. Okay, a lot. Suddenly, she wanted to go home, where it was safe. She was about to tell Seth that when he set down his cue and eyed her.

"You're bored."

If he only knew how unbored she was. How badly she wanted him. "Not at all," she said. "I'm just worried about everything I need to do before the fund-raiser."

"Uh-uh." He wagged his finger at her. "There'll be no more thinking about that tonight." He grabbed her cue from its place against the wall and handed it to her. "Your turn."

"But you haven't missed yet."

"That's okay. Go ahead and chalk up, and I'll teach you some pool tricks."

Moments later, he stood behind her. Reaching around, he covered her hands with his. She could feel the heat from his solid frame and the warmth of his breath against her ear. Her body went soft inside and her heart just about thudded out of her chest.

"Bend down a little, so you're almost at eye level with the table," he said, guiding her into position.

Now his groin was flush with her rear end. Emily could feel his arousal. Barely able to form a coherent thought, she stammered, "N-now what?"

"Keep your eye on the ball, and aim for where you want it to go."

His lips grazed her ear when he spoke, and a delicious shiver ran up her spine.

"Which ball first?" he asked, his voice gruff.

"R-red."

"Line it up. Aim. Go for it."

He stepped back, taking his warmth with him.

Emily missed. "Shoot," she said.

But Seth wasn't looking at the wayward red ball or the table. His hot eyes roved over her, heating her everywhere they touched. After pausing for a smoldering look at her mouth, he met her gaze with unconcealed need. She could no more look away than fly.

"Game's over," he said.

"You don't want to finish it?"

His eyes grew hooded and he shook his head. "Let's get out of here."

EMILY WAS SILENT as she and Seth made their way to the street where he'd parked. He kept his arm around her. The breath chuffed from his lips in clouds that mingled with her own.

In her mind, she waged a silent battle. *Yes, be with him tonight. No, protect yourself and hug a pillow instead.*

As soon they reached the pickup, he braced her against the passenger side, plowed his fingers up under the back of her hair and kissed her. Gently at first, then deeper and with more urgency.

When her legs could barely support her, he broke the kiss. "I want you," he growled.

Although Emily felt the same about him, she was also conflicted. She bit her lip. "I've never had sex outside of a relationship."

"I thought... Seems like you... Oh, hell, I misread things. I'll take you home."

He unlocked her door and she climbed in. While he walked around the driver's side, she thought about what she really wanted. Her mind assured her that going home was the safe thing to do, but her heart and body didn't want that.

It was all so confusing.

The engine purred to life. Seth adjusted the heat. He was reaching to release the parking brake when she placed her hand on his forearm. Eyeing her, he sat back.

"I don't want to leave like this, Seth. I want to be with you, but I'm nervous."

His eyes seemed to glow with heat. "One of the things I like most about you and me is that we're straight with each other. Okay."

Their relationship, if Emily could call it that, was so different from what she'd shared with Harvey. He'd lied about loving her and about always being there for her. But with Seth, she knew up front that he wasn't interested in love. He respected her enough to be frank, and that meant a great deal to her.

Cupping her shoulders, he turned her in her seat to face him. "As bad as I want to make love with you tonight, I think we should wait until you're sure about this."

"But now is the perfect time," she argued, because she wanted him so much. "Taylor's gone all night, and you don't have to worry about her. We won't get this chance again."

"Yeah, we will. There'll be other overnights."

She laughed self-consciously. "Are you trying to talk us out of being together tonight?"

Somber and intent, he tipped up her chin. "Make no mistake, Emily—I burn to be buried deep inside of you. But not if you have doubts. I want this to be good for both of us. And when it finally happens, it'll be dynamite."

His patience and understanding awed her. She'd never met a man like him, had never felt such hunger for anyone.

But what about the risks to her heart?

In the end, her desire drowned out the fear of falling for him. "Your house or mine?" she asked.

"Don't mess with me."

"I wouldn't tease about this."

He gave her a long, searching look. Apparently what he saw in her eyes satisfied him, for he nodded. "My place is closer."

On the drive to his house, he turned on the radio. A woman with an amazing voice was singing about her broken heart. Emily wasn't about to let her heart get broken. Tonight was about slaking the hunger that wouldn't go away, nothing more.

It seemed like no time before Seth pulled into the carport and opened her door.

The drapes in the house had been pulled against the night, and lamplight blazed inside. He unlocked the side door off the carport and stepped back, letting her precede him. They stepped into a small entryway. Emily barely had time to glance at the couch and matching armchairs in the living room before he ripped off his coat and removed hers. Right there in the entryway, he kissed her.

"You smell so sweet," he said, when they came up for air. "Like honeysuckle. A breath of summer in the cold of winter."

Dazed with desire, she could barely speak. "I'm trying a new shampoo."

"Keep using it."

He went back to kissing her, and for some time she lost herself in his warmth and the scent and taste that were uniquely his.

When they pulled back again, they were both breathing hard.

"Before we go any further…" Seth brushed strands of hair out of her face. "Are you sure about this? If not, tell me now, and I'll take you home."

Emily was positive. As long as she kept her heart safe…

He tucked her hair behind her ears, skimmed his thumbs across her cheeks, leaving a trail of heat everywhere he touched her.

"I'm sure." She wrapped her arms around his neck. "Make love with me, Seth."

Chapter Sixteen

Eager to get Emily into bed, Seth tugged her toward the stairs. They didn't make it far before he stopped to taste her and nuzzle the sensitive place where her neck curved into her shoulder. She shivered in his arms.

She was incredibly responsive and eager, and he'd never wanted a woman so much. He kissed her again. She responed with a passion that went straight to his groin, and he almost lost control right there on the steps. But she deserved better.

By the time they reached the second floor, they'd lost their shoes and their shirts. In the bedroom, he switched on the bedside table lamp, then tore off the bedspread and tossed it aside.

Locking her eyes on him, Emily unfastened her bra. It slid from her shoulders and dropped to the floor. The nipples of her small, perfect breasts were already swollen and rigid.

Recapturing the mouth he couldn't get enough of, he eased her onto the bed. Some time later, he left her lips for her breasts, licking and tasting until she was gasping and restless. Wanting her naked, he unfastened the button on her jeans and pulled the zipper. "Let's get rid of these."

"Yours, too," she said.

They made short work of disposing of their remaining clothing. Seth looked his fill at the beautiful, willing woman waiting for him. Flushed skin, kiss-swollen lips, eyes bright with hunger.

His.

He explored her rib cage with his mouth and his hands. Her navel. As he slowly moved lower, she swallowed audibly and shifted restlessly. He slid his palms up her petal-soft inner thighs, which opened readily. Even before he parted her slick folds, she was lifting her hips. "Please, Seth."

"Is this what you want?" He touched her most sensitive part with his tongue.

"Oh, sweet heaven."

He'd barely begun before she pushed him away. "Too soft, too hard?" he asked.

"Not enough. I need you inside me."

She didn't have to ask twice. "Give me a sec." He moved away, opened a foil packet and put on the condom. When he returned to Emily, she held out her arms.

Seth covered her with his body, and in one slick move, slid into her warmth. *Home.*

"This—you—feel so good," he said. He wanted to go slowly and make their first time together last, but she was frantic and active, gripping his hips with her thighs and squeezing him with her inner muscles.

"Easy," he warned through gritted teeth. "Or this will be over way too soon."

"I *want* soon. I want now."

With that, he lost control, pushing deeper and faster until the world blurred and nothing mattered but completing the act with Emily. She cried out and they soared together, in a long, shuddering climax that shook him to the core.

Blown away by the intensity of the pleasure they'd just shared, he rolled to his side and brought her with him.

When he came back to earth, he kissed her lightly on the lips. "Told you we'd be dynamite in bed."

Rosy-skinned and looking thoroughly loved, she let out a satisfied sigh. "That was…wow. There really are no words."

"Any regrets?"

"None." She smiled drowsily.

They understood each other perfectly—best feeling in the world. Grinning, he pulled her against his side.

They both went quiet, and Seth thought she might fall asleep. Keeping his arm around her, he switched off the lamp with his free hand. He stared into the darkness. He liked having Emily beside him in his bed. A lot.

He cupped her smooth hip, and she snuggled closer, all warm and willing and sweet. Yep, he could definitely get used to this. Emily in his bed, every night…

Seth quickly squelched that thought, for several reasons. With his track record, he was sure to mess things up, and she'd been hurt enough. Then there was Taylor. Now that their relationship had finally turned the corner, he needed to make sure they continued to move forward. Add in his practice, which was finally expanding, and there wasn't time for a serious relationship.

It was a relief that Emily didn't want that, either.

They would see each other when they could, and leave it at that. His eyes drifted shut and he dozed off.

SETH'S BREATHING WAS slow and even, signaling that he was asleep. Sated and relaxed, Emily was ready for sleep, too. Thoughts drifted through her mind. Lovemaking had never been like this. Seth had made her feel desired, beautiful and cherished—complete.

His hand tightened on her hip, sweetly and possessively. Feelings flooded her—warmth and joy and a feeling dangerously close to…love.

No, not love!

Emily started to panic. If Seth had given any indication that his feelings had deepened, she might be, shock of shocks, willing to take the risk and give him her heart. But he'd made it clear that he didn't have the time or interest for love.

She needed to go home. Now.

She untangled her limbs from Seth's and woke him. "I

should get back. Susannah's probably pacing the apartment, and what if one of the other dogs needs me?"

"Okay." Seth flipped on the lamp.

By the time they collected scattered clothing and dressed, it was almost midnight. Emily was sitting in a chair, pulling on her boots, and Seth was scooping their coats from the floor where they'd dropped them in their haste to make love, when the front door clicked.

"What the hell?" he muttered.

Emily scrambled to her feet—just as Taylor walked in.

At the sight of them, the girl stopped in her tracks, eyes wide with surprise.

"Hey," Seth said.

He'd pulled on a T-shirt but had left his flannel shirt unbuttoned. Certain that she looked equally rumpled, Emily smoothed her hair.

Taylor turned an accusing glare at her guardian. "I tried to call you to pick me up, but you didn't answer. Cat's dad had to drive me home."

"I, uh, didn't hear the phone. I thought tonight was a sleepover."

"It was supposed to be, but Cat… We had a fight."

"Oh, no," Emily said. "What happened?"

"I don't want to talk about it." Taylor shoved her bangs out of her face and scowled at Seth. "You said you weren't dating Emily. Why can't you ever tell me the truth?"

He blew out a loud breath. "We did go out tonight, but it wasn't planned. Otherwise, I would have told you. This was a spur of the moment thing."

"That's exactly what you said the last time." Taylor looked pretty unhappy.

"Are you upset that Seth and I went out?" Emily asked.

"No. I just… Why doesn't anyone ever tell me anything?" The girl's eyes filled with tears, which she hastily brushed away.

"I tell you stuff all the time," Seth said. "And I don't lie to you. Ever."

Emily nodded. "I'll vouch for that. If you ever want to talk about anything, I'm here for you."

Taylor hung her head, and Emily realized she needed more, some kind of explanation about tonight. "You want to know what happened?" she said. *I think I'm falling for Seth.* "Suddenly you had plans, but Seth didn't. Neither did I. We had this crazy idea to go out and play pool." Hoping to make the girl smile, Emily added, "He's good and I stink, so you know how that ended."

Unfortunately, Taylor seemed to find nothing funny in that.

"When the game ended, I wasn't ready to go home yet," Emily went on. "So we came back here for a while." She gestured at their coats. "Seth was about to drive me to my house."

He nodded. "It's late, and Emily needs to get home. You and I will finish this conversation when I get back."

"I'm tired. I'll be asleep." Taylor turned away and started for the stairs.

"Hold it right there. Say good-night to Emily."

Taylor stopped and stiffened her spine before she pivoted to face them. "Good night, Emily."

Emily ignored the exaggerated politeness. "Night, Taylor. I'll see you next Thursday."

With a terse nod, the girl spun around and hurried up the stairs.

"That went well," Seth muttered as he backed out of the carport. He hadn't seen Taylor this upset in weeks. "I thought she'd be okay now if you and I went out. Wrong."

"You should probably talk to her again about that," Emily said. "But I'm pretty sure she's more rattled by what happened with Cat. They'll make up."

"They'd better. Taylor needs all the friends she can get. What do you think happened?"

Emily shook her head. "With teenagers, it could be anything. It must have been a pretty bad fight, or Taylor wouldn't have come home. She was already angry. Then she walks into the house and finds you and me alone. I can't imagine what she must be thinking."

"For starters, that I lied to her about dating you." That stung. "I wish to God that she trusted me."

"I'm sure that in time, she will. It's a good thing we straightened up the bed."

"And that we weren't still *in* it."

Emily turned on the radio, and for the rest of the drive, they listened in silence to oldies. In Seth's mind, he replayed the evening. He and Emily, talking and laughing at the pool hall. Taking her to his bed and loving her.

Then the thing with Taylor. As soon as he got back home, he would find out what had happened tonight, and make her understand about him and Emily. For now, as much as he hated seeing her mad, it was a relief that for once, Cat shared the hot seat.

He pulled up in front of the shelter and let the engine idle. "I enjoyed tonight—all except the very last part."

"So did I."

Her hair was messy, her lips still a little swollen from their loving. Such a passionate, beautiful woman. He wanted her even more than before. "I want to see you again," he said. "Soon."

Soft light warmed her eyes. "Oh, Seth, I..." Cutting herself off, she caught her bottom lip between her teeth in a telltale sign of uncertainty. "But what about Taylor? Don't you want to focus on her and building your practice?"

"Of course, and I intend to make sure she understands that. But I need more than that in my life. You and I laugh together. We get along great and neither of us is looking for anything deep. Why shouldn't we see each other?"

She blinked and the warmth vanished. "With the fund-raiser coming up and so much to do…I can't."

The surprising reply caught him off guard. Before he could react, she opened the passenger door.

"Good night, Seth." Without a backward glance, she slipped out of the truck.

Confused, he shook his head. What had just happened?

Chapter Seventeen

Lots of tasks needed Emily's attention Monday afternoon, but a bad case of stress made focusing difficult. Unable to sit still, she stood and stared out her office window. Attuned to her mood, Susannah stuck close by, studying her with worried eyes.

"I'm fine," she soothed, but the dog wasn't buying it.

The reason for her anxiety? Later this afternoon, a new dog was coming in, and she needed to contact Seth.

They hadn't spoken since Saturday night, which was both a relief and a disappointment.

He had asked to see her again. His intent gaze had almost convinced her that he'd changed his mind and wanted a deeper relationship. Fool that she was, she'd been ready to hand over her heart. Then he'd made it nice and clear that he wasn't interested in serious.

He assumed she felt the same way—after all, only hours earlier, she'd assured him of that. The trouble was she no longer did.

If only she'd stayed home and worked Saturday night. Emily scoffed. As if that would have made a difference. The truth was, even if she'd hidden away upstairs, she would still be in a world of trouble.

Susannah licked her hand in canine sympathy. "I know you like him, too," Emily said.

All the dogs did. As wonderful as he was at doctoring them, right now she wished he wasn't the shelter vet. Because if she didn't have to see or talk to him, forgetting him would be easier.

She no longer wanted him to stay on as the vet here, and he certainly didn't want to. Time to pull her head out of the sand. "As soon as this fund-raiser is over, I'll concentrate on finding a replacement veterinarian," she added.

Which was all well and good, but didn't change the fact that she needed to let Seth know about the new dog. With a heavy sigh, she picked up the phone.

He didn't answer, and she left a message. She was organizing the list of donations various businesses had offered, when she heard the bell over the front door.

"Taylor," Mrs. Oakes said, her voice carrying into Emily's office. "This is a surprise. We don't usually see you except on Thursdays."

"I need to speak with Emily."

Wondering if she was here to get angry about her and Seth, or talk about Cat, or something else entirely, Emily stood. Then Taylor entered her office.

"Hi." Emily didn't bother with a forced smile, just gazed at the girl with what she hoped was an open expression.

"Hi." Avoiding eye contact, Taylor bent to the task of greeting Susannah.

"I heard you tell Mrs. Oakes you wanted to talk?"

Taylor nodded, shut the door and took a chair across the desk.

"If this is about the other night…" Unsure what to say, Emily let the words trail off.

Taylor looked surprised. "How did you know?"

"I thought Seth explained again after he took me home."

"Huh?" Understanding dawned on her face. "Oh, you mean you and him. We didn't talk about that, or anything else. I can't talk to him."

"You most certainly can."

"Maybe I don't want to. Since you brought it up, are you and Seth together now?"

"No." Emily shook her head. "We're both really busy.

I've got this fund-raiser and the shelter and my website business. And Seth…" He didn't want love.

Before she could go on, Taylor gave a satisfied nod. "Good."

"You don't like us to see each other outside the shelter," Emily said, just to clarify.

"Not really."

Then her decision was for best. Still, she needed to find out more. "May I ask why?"

"Because… I didn't come here to talk about that." Taylor gave her a surly look.

"Still, I'd like to know."

"Because then…"

The girl's lips clamped shut, and for a long moment Emily didn't think she'd answer. Just in case, she remained silent.

After a moment, Taylor glanced down at her hands. "Because then you'll both forget that I exist," she said, in a voice so soft Emily barely heard the words.

Emily's heart ached for her. She also wondered why Taylor would think such a thing. "Oh, honey, neither of us could ever do that. You're too special for me to forget, and I happen to know that you are Seth's main focus."

Taylor made a sound of disbelief.

"He really cares about you," Emily explained.

The girl's eyes narrowed suspiciously. "He said that?"

"All the time. You should hear the way he talks about you. You mean the world to him. He wants you to be happy."

Doubt colored Taylor's expression, before her face went blank. "If that's true, why won't he take me back to San Diego?"

"Because you live in Prosperity."

"I hate it here!"

The forceful tone shocked Emily. "I don't know what to say, Taylor, other than this is your home now."

"I *knew* you'd side with him. Forget it." She stood to leave.

Feeling completely out of her element, Emily sighed. "Please don't leave like this, Taylor."

To her relief, the girl plopped back down. But she didn't speak.

Emily guessed she needed to get the ball rolling. "What happened at Cat's the other night?"

"I do *not* want to talk about that or her," Taylor stated flatly.

Ah. "You're still in a fight."

"No duh. That's why I'm here. Can I start coming on Tuesdays instead of Thursdays?"

Emily didn't even have to pause to think about that. "That's when Matt and Shayna volunteer. I need you on Thursdays."

Taylor tugged on her jacket sleeve. "But I don't want to work with Cat anymore."

"You've been such good friends. Don't you think you should talk and make up?"

"What for? She doesn't care about me. She only cares about *Isaac*." Taylor sneered the name as if it were something distasteful.

"Who's Isaac?"

"A boy we met when we were getting businesses to donate for the silent auction. He and Cat had a date Friday night. Now they're going out. All they do is text and talk on FaceTime."

She sounded jealous. Emily gave her a sideways look. "Does Isaac have anything to do with what happened Saturday night?"

With that question, Taylor dropped the *I don't want to talk about that* pose and poured out her heart. "I don't even know why she invited me over. She sure didn't want to hang out with me. At least not after Isaac contacted her. All she wanted to do was talk to him."

"That doesn't sound like much fun for you."

Taylor glanced at the floor, as if meeting Emily's gaze might cause her to fall apart. "She took her phone into the bathroom and locked the door. I waited in her bedroom. Where else would I go—downstairs with her parents?" Taylor rolled her eyes.

"Is that when you tried to call Seth?" Emily asked.

"No. For a while, I talked to a friend in San Diego, but she had to go. I knocked on the bathroom door, and told Cat that if she didn't want me around, I'd leave. She said to go ahead."

Despite Taylor's *who cares* shrug, pain clouded her eyes. Emily wanted to comfort her with a touch or a hug, but sensed that she simply wanted a friendly ear.

"I know how you feel," Emily said. "Something similar happened to me once, when I was a little older than you. I didn't date much in high school, and neither did my best friend, Andrea. Then she met Gene, a boy from a different school. He asked her out, and before long, they were spending all their spare time together. Andrea didn't have room in her life for me anymore."

One more person Emily cared about had deserted her— at least at the time, that's how she'd interpreted what had happened. She remembered feeling mad and jealous, but most of all, alone.

She had Taylor's full attention. "What did you do?"

"I'd lost my best friend, and I was miserable. Even worse, we were in a lot of the same classes. We'd always sat together, and the teachers had made up their seating charts that way. Which meant we were stuck in our usual seats. Things were pretty tense. We didn't look at or speak to each other, and boy, was that uncomfortable."

Talking about it brought back some of the pain and helped Emily understand what Taylor was going through. "A few weeks later Andrea and Gene broke up. She was really sad, and she called me. I went over to her house and we hugged and cried and talked. We decided that no boy would ever come between us again, and promised to always make time for each other."

"And did you?"

"Pretty much. During those last two years of high school, Andrea must have had five or six boyfriends. I dated a few guys and had an after-school job. But we still talked almost every day, and we managed to get together once or twice a week. When it was time for us to go to college, Andrea moved to Missoula. I stayed here and commuted to the local community college. Her junior year, she started dating a guy from Missoula. When she graduated, she stayed there to be with him. They're married now, with three kids. But she and I are still friends. So take heart—things will work out between you and Cat."

"I don't think Cat wants to be friends anymore." Taylor hung her head.

"I'll bet she does. Why don't you give it a few more days and then talk to her?"

"You mean on Thursday afternoon," Taylor said with a shrewd look. "You're just trying to get me to come back on my usual day."

Smart girl. "Partly," Emily admitted. "I need your help getting ready for the fund-raiser, and I also want you and Cat to make up. You're too good of friends to let some boy get in the way." The office phone rang. "I should probably answer this," she said. "It could be about the new dog that's coming in this afternoon. But don't go yet."

She answered the phone and heard the masculine voice she knew so well. "Hey, it's Seth."

Her traitorous heart lifted. "Hi, Seth," she said, for Taylor's benefit.

The girl signaled Emily not to let on that she was there. Emily nodded.

"When do you expect the new dog?" he asked.

"He'll probably be here sometime in the next one to

two hours. Then I'll need time to admit him and get him settled."

"Perfect—I'm booked up until around five," Seth said.

"Feel free to come after that, or even tomorrow morning."

"Later today works better for me. I'm still thinking about the other night." His tone became low and intimate.

Emily's body responded instantly, going hot with longing. She pivoted her chair around so that her back was to Taylor and the girl couldn't see her expression. "Me, too," she admitted.

"I knew it. Look, I know you're busy—we both are. But using the fund-raiser as an excuse not to see me again? Come on, Em. We agreed to be honest with each other."

She wasn't about to discuss that now. "Why don't we talk when you get here."

"That's all I ask. See you in a couple of hours."

Emily disconnected and pivoted the chair around. She couldn't read Taylor's expression. "We're getting a new dog anytime now, and Seth will be over after his appointments to examine it," she said. "If you want to do your homework and wait for him—"

"No!" Taylor shook her head and jumped up. "I don't want him to know I was here. I need to go."

"But how will you get home?"

"There's a late bus for kids who stay for after-school activities. I'll catch that."

"Okay." Emily walked her to the door. "So I'll see you Thursday?"

"Sure," Taylor said, but she wouldn't make eye contact.

Vaguely uneasy, Emily returned to her office.

JESSIE AND BIRCH, two of the other community service volunteers from Trenton, were on the after-school bus. They greeted Taylor, but headed toward the rear without inviting her to join them. She was used to that. Anyway, she didn't feel much like making conversation.

The bus was less than half full, and she slid into an empty seat in front, where she stared out the window at the gray afternoon. She felt kind of gray, too.

She wasn't sure what Seth had said to Emily on the phone, but she could tell it was something about the two of them. No matter what Emily said, it was easy to see that they were into each other. She'd even turned her back on Taylor to talk to him.

Taylor knew what that meant. She'd been through it with her mom too many times. Having a boyfriend meant that she was forgotten. Hadn't it just happened with Cat?

That stuff Emily had told her about being special? Ha. And Andrea? Nice story, but it didn't apply to Taylor.

Guys were the same way. When they were into a girl, they didn't see Taylor anymore. Now that Seth liked Emily, he was bound to forget she existed, just like before.

Once again, she was alone. Unwanted. Her shoulders slumped. She thought about San Diego and the friends there who cared about her.

And came to a decision. She would run away and stay with them.

That'd show Seth, Emily and Cat. Taylor didn't need any of them.

She sat up straighter, until she thought about how she was going to get there. She didn't have the money for a plane or a bus ticket. Well, she wouldn't let that stop her. She would borrow from her friends and pay them back later.

During the last few minutes of the bus ride, she pulled out her phone and texted Kayla and Hanna, letting them know what she needed.

As soon as they sent the money, she would leave for good.

Chapter Eighteen

After stewing—should she tell Seth Taylor had been there and that she was worried, or keep her confidence?—Emily connected with Monica and Bridget on a three-way call for advice.

She updated them on Seth—on everything from what had happened Saturday night, to the talk he expected to have when he stopped by later. Then she filled them in about Taylor.

"What do I do?" she asked.

Monica, who was still seeing Bart, the man she'd met at the bowling alley, laughed. "For starters, knock some sense into your head. Seth is a honey. Tell him you changed your mind and that you want to see him, after all."

"I agree," Bridget said. "He likes you."

"That's just it—he *likes* me," Emily replied. "He wants to keep our relationship casual. I told him that I do, too, but the trouble is I'm falling for him."

"It's about time," Bridget said. "I envy you."

"Well, don't. I'm not happy about this."

"Can't you two just relax and let it all unfold?" Monica asked. "That's what Bart and I are doing."

"I don't see that happening with Seth and me."

"Because you're scared."

Emily wasn't going to argue with that. How could she, when it was true?

"You know where fear will get you," Bridget said. "Two words—*Aunt Arlene*."

Emily glanced up and shook her head, but of course,

her friends couldn't see her. "We all know I have issues with getting involved again, but let's move on," she said. "I'm not sure what to do about Taylor. Do I tell Seth that she stopped by today, and what she said?"

"If I was a teenage girl and I told an adult about a problem with a friend and then she blabbed about it to either of my parents, I'd be furious," Bridget said.

"I agree," Monica seconded. "Teenage girls are drama queens. By tomorrow, Taylor and her friend will probably be thick as thieves again."

"Maybe I'll hold off, then," Emily said. "Or maybe not. I think I'll play it by ear." Downstairs, the bell over the door jingled. "Oops, the new dog is here—gotta run."

"Keep us posted," Monica said.

BY THE TIME Seth showed up, Emily was pretty much a nervous wreck. First and foremost because of the talk he expected to have. When she'd explained that she was too busy to see him the other night, it had been dark, and as soon as she uttered the words, she'd hurried inside. Telling him again, face-to-face and in a lighted room, seemed a lot more daunting. Mainly because Seth Pettit was a hard man to resist. But her heart was at risk, and for her own good she needed to convince him that she meant it.

Then there was Taylor and what to do about her. A part of Emily agreed with Monica and Bridget that the whole drama would soon pass. Plus, she didn't want to risk alienating the girl. Yet at the same time, a nagging feeling she couldn't shake urged her to share her concerns with Seth.

"You seem tense," he said after she let him in. "I'm not trying to pressure you into seeing me if you don't want to, but I want to know what changed the other night between my place and yours."

"Well, I…"

The warm, intent gaze that made her long for the things Seth wasn't interested in giving searched her face. Not about to admit that she was afraid of her own feelings, she glanced down. "It's difficult to explain."

"This is about the sex." He massaged his forehead, as if he had a headache. "I knew we should have waited."

Emily hadn't wanted to. "I'm not at all sorry it happened, Seth."

"It—*we*—were phenomenal."

His hot look melted her, but she steeled herself against her feelings. "I really am busy," she said. "Volunteers can only do so much. This is my fund-raiser, and everything needs my okay. Plus there are details that I need to handle myself, like organizing the donations, and the countless little things that pop up. We're a small organization, with under two hundred people expected at the fund-raiser, but pulling it all together is still a huge job."

Seth opened his mouth, but Emily didn't want to hear whatever it was he would say. She hurried on. "Speaking of the fund-raiser, I really need to get some stuff done tonight. I got the new dog settled in about an hour ago, and he's waiting."

"Fine—change the subject and blow me off." Aggravation flared in Seth's eyes, and he waved his hand in a curt gesture. "Go on and get to work, then. I'll examine the dog and email my report."

Now she felt terrible. "I'm not blowing you off, Seth. I'll work after you leave. Let me grab my coat and come with you."

They headed for the quarantine hut. Snow swirled around them, large flakes that reminded her of Taylor's first experience with snow. Emily didn't want to ruin the relationship with her by betraying her trust, but...

"Emily? You're a million miles away. I said, tell me about the dog." His cool voice and body language were all business now, as if they'd never been anything but shelter owner and volunteer veterinarian.

Although this was exactly what she assured herself she

wanted, she didn't like it. She was so mixed up. "He's young, maybe a few years old, with poodle and black lab in him," she said. "His eyes are blue, and I'm guessing he's also part collie or husky. He's pretty upset. It took me and two volunteers to get him into a cage. I'm worried about Taylor," she blurted out.

Instantly, Seth warmed to her again, and her heart lifted in relief.

"She's in a bad place, that's for sure. Sunday was dismal, and so was this morning. For a little while there, I felt sure we were making progress. Now it's almost as bad as when we first moved to Prosperity." He blew out a breath. "For every step she takes forward, she seems to take two back. But I don't think this is about you and me. I'm pretty sure it's about Cat. I wish I knew what happened."

He needed insights, and Taylor needed help. Emily had to step up—even if the girl would be angry. "Taylor doesn't want me to tell you this, and I hate breaking her confidence, but this is important. She stopped by after school today."

They entered the hut, which felt cozy and warm after the cold night air.

"Hold that thought until I examine this dog."

Like most of the other shelter animals, this one snarled and bared his teeth. Unlike the others, he wouldn't allow Seth to approach the cage, even with the offer of a doggy treat. Growling a fierce warning, the dog leaped at the bars, banging the cage hard in an attempt to get out.

"If I'm going to examine him tonight, I'll have to sedate him first," Seth said in a low voice. "You know the drill."

Emily mixed a sedative with a small amount of food, then, using a long-handled spatula, placed the bowl in the cage. The dog ignored it until Seth and Emily moved to the corner, which in the small hut was as far away from the cage as they could get.

It took nearly fifteen minutes before he gobbled down the food.

"Finally," Seth murmured. "While we wait for the drug to take effect, tell me why Taylor came by today."

"As I said earlier, she won't like that I told you, but I have to. She asked to switch her community-service day to Tuesday, so she can avoid Cat."

Seth whistled. "That's one doozy of a fight."

"It's more of a misunderstanding, and it revolves around a boy named Isaac."

"Taylor has a boyfriend?" Seth didn't look happy about that.

"Not Taylor—Cat. Apparently, she'd rather be on Face-Time with Isaac than be with Taylor. That's what happened Saturday night. Cat ended up telling Taylor to go home."

"No wonder she's been so upset." His eyes narrowed a fraction, as they often did when he was thinking. "Why the hell did Cat invite her over?"

"Maybe she hadn't planned to talk with Isaac that night."

"Teenagers." Seth shook his head. "It's a miracle any-one survives those years. Are you going to let her switch to Tuesdays?"

"No. Two other kids come in that day. I suggested she work things out with Cat."

"But you're worried she won't."

"Who knows? They're teenage girls. What makes me nervous is that Taylor seemed…removed. Nothing I can put my finger on, but I get the feeling that she won't show up on Thursday. Oh, and she also mentioned moving back to San Diego."

"Not that again. I'll talk to her, and I'll make sure she shows up when she's supposed to."

"She's going to be upset that I told you."

"I'll keep that in mind." Seth glanced toward the cage. "He seems to be more relaxed now."

But not by much. As they neared the cage, the dog growled and snarled and butted the bars hard. He wasn't going to cooperate. Emily was glad she'd accompanied

Seth, because he needed two extra hands to help muzzle and hold him still during the exam.

"He seems in okay shape right now, but I see evidence of abuse," Seth said, pointing out old whip scars. "We'd better bathe him now, before the sedative wears off."

They both ended up wet and sustained a few scratches, but they managed the job. They dried the animal as best they could, removed the muzzle and returned him safely to his cage. After toweling themselves off, they donned their coats and headed back to the office. The snow was coming down harder now.

"The roads will be slick," Emily warned. "You'd better leave now, or you might not make it."

Seth nodded. "I'll get back to you with the lab test results. If you change your mind about us…"

He started to reach out and touch her face, but dropped his hand instead.

Then he was gone.

BEFORE HEADING FOR HOME, Seth sat in the truck at the end of the shelter's driveway and phoned Harper's for a pizza to go. Dinner. On the way to the restaurant, the snow and patches of black ice coating the road took all his focus. Once he had the pizza, he headed carefully for home. He was tired, hungry and out of sorts. Mainly because Emily had stuck to her decision. She wasn't going to see him outside the shelter.

Dammit, he liked her. He didn't buy her *I'm too busy* excuse, but he couldn't force her to share the real reason she'd changed her mind. What choice did he have but to let her be?

From now on, he was the shelter's volunteer veterinarian, period. Being around her was bound to be awkward, but he'd given his word to stay until Taylor completed her community service. The day she finished, want to or not, he would go his separate way and probably not see Emily again.

Now he had to deal with Taylor.

As usual, she was upstairs. He knocked on her bedroom door. "I brought home an extra large pepperoni and chicken pizza with pineapple—your favorite."

"I don't want any."

He'd figured as much, but was in no mood for her shenanigans. No kid gloves tonight. He opened her door. "Then you can watch me eat. You're coming downstairs, and we're going to talk over dinner."

She gave him a look that could kill—eyes flashing, mouth in a thin line. But she came out.

In silence, they washed up. Taylor got herself a pop, and Seth opened a beer.

He set out the plates and napkins, and then pointed at her chair in the breakfast nook. They both sat down. Seth dug in.

After all of two seconds, she relented. "I guess I'll eat."

Getting tough seemed to have worked. He smiled to himself.

He waited until they'd both slowed down before he started. "You haven't said two words to me since Saturday night. If you still hate me, that's your choice. But I'm not taking you back to San Diego. You can't just run away from your problems."

She looked suspicious. "Have you been checking my texts?"

"I wouldn't do that. Why, should I be?"

"Don't you dare!" She eyed him. "Emily told you I came in today, didn't she?"

Not about to lie, he nodded.

"I asked her not to say anything!"

"And she feels bad about that. She only said something because she's worried about you."

Taylor's upper lip curled. "Yeah, right."

"What's that supposed to mean?"

"I was there when you called this afternoon. I know what's going on with you and her."

As of midnight Saturday night, nothing at all. He scowled. "And what exactly is that?"

"You like each other."

Emily *had* liked him, but not anymore. Seth snorted. "What's that got to do with her being worried about you?"

"I don't know how she could be. She doesn't have time for me, and neither do you. No one does!"

With her dramatic flair, Taylor could write for the soaps. "Of course I do," he said in a reasonable tone. "So does Emily. By the way, from now on, she and I won't be seeing each other outside of the shelter."

"That's what she said, but I don't believe her."

"You don't have to, but it's true. And FYI, just because two people are involved doesn't mean they forget someone as important as you."

"She said that, too." Taylor snickered and crossed her arms, but the vulnerability beneath that glare…

Seth figured this particular issue had nothing to do with Cat or with him and Emily. "I get the feeling this has happened to you before," he said.

One shoulder lifted and fell.

He'd bet the four new ranches he'd added to his practice that this was about Annabelle. He knew how she'd been with him at first, lost in the newness of his moving in, but he also knew that her feelings for Taylor had never diminished. "People get weird when they're in love," he said, "but that doesn't mean they stop loving everyone else."

Doubt crept into Taylor's eyes, before she put on her stubborn face. "They sure act that way."

"I know. But trust me, you matter. Got that?" He waited for her terse nod before continuing. "I expect you to go to community service on Thursday."

"But I don't want to see Cat!"

"You made a commitment, and you're going." He didn't like the defiant look on her face. "I can always pick you up at school and drop you off there." He knew she'd hate that.

"No way. I'll walk over, like I always do. But only because you're making me."

He responded to her dirty look with a benign nod. "Thank you."

"YOU TOLD SETH I was here on Monday!" Taylor exploded when she marched through the shelter door Thursday afternoon. "You said you wouldn't!"

Mrs. Oakes glanced at Emily with a *teenage girls—what can you do?* expression.

But Emily felt terrible. "I apologize," she said. "I did it because Seth was worried about you, and so was I. Will you forgive me?"

Taylor's only response was a stony look.

Today wasn't going to be easy. "I'm so glad you're here," Emily soothed. "With the fund-raiser next week, I could really use your help."

"Like I had a choice."

The bell above the door jingled, and Cat strolled into the front office. The surly look she shot Taylor was enough to make Emily cringe, but Taylor studiously ignored her friend. The tension between them was so thick that Emily could almost reach out and touch it.

The girls were mad at each other, and Taylor was angry with her. Wonderful.

With this afternoon's full agenda, Emily couldn't afford to wait for them to make up on their own. Ignoring the animosity swirling through the room, she greeted Cat with a smile. "Now that you're both here, follow me."

She led them to the kitchen and gestured at the table. "This afternoon, you're going to decorate cards for each of the items donated to our silent auction."

"I can do that," Cat said, as if Taylor wasn't in the room. "What kinds of decorations are you thinking?"

"That's up to you. Each item has its own card and needs a design that will draw attention and, hopefully, bids.

"For example." Emily picked up a card from the stack. "This is one of the items from Dani Kelly and Big Mama. 'Free brunch for six from Big Mama's Café,'" she read. "Your job is to make the card look enticing. Art supplies are in the cupboard to the right of the sink."

"I'm on it." Cat headed for the cupboard.

"What about me?" Taylor asked, pointedly glancing away from the other girl.

"You and Cat will be working on this together."

Neither looked happy. With grudging nods, they pulled out supplies. Crossing her fingers that they'd finally make up, Emily left them alone.

Some two and a half hours later, Taylor handed the finished cards to Emily for review. Cat plunked herself onto the couch and checked her phone.

They still had roughly thirty minutes before their rides arrived. Not enough time to start a new chore, but they needed something to do. Suddenly, Emily had an idea.

"We got a new dog on Monday," she said. "The lab tests came back okay, but Seth and I believe he was abused. He could use some company."

"I'll go," Taylor said.

Cat frowned. "Hey, I wanted to do it."

"Why don't you both visit him?" Emily suggested. "Be aware, though, that he is hypersensitive. He needs positive, loving people around him. You'll have to put that anger aside."

"Whatever," Taylor muttered.

Cat shrugged.

The grudging agreement wasn't ideal, but better than their blatant hostility of before. "If you move too close, he gets upset, so just sit and be with him."

Without glancing at each other, the girls headed off.

By the time Seth arrived, both Mrs. Oakes and Cat had left.

Pretending not to care for him was just as difficult now as it had been Monday night. Emily managed a smile. "Hi."

He gave a terse nod. "Where's Taylor?"

"In the kennel, sitting with the new dog. She's pretty mad at me for telling you about her and Cat." Emily bit her lip. "I hate that. I tried to explain that I was concerned, but she didn't want to listen."

"She'll get over it. What about Cat?"

"She's upset, too, but not with me. She went home a few minutes ago. I made the girls work together on decorations for the silent auction. Then they both sat with the dog. I wouldn't let them visit him until they agreed to put aside their anger."

"And did they?" When Emily nodded, Seth shook his head. "No kidding." For a moment he lost some of his stiffness and looked impressed. "You're saying they're friends again?"

"Judging by their behavior, I don't think so."

"Bummer, but I'll bet they will be. You're amaz— I appreciate the update," he said, distant again. "I'll get Taylor and we'll be off." He turned away and walked back outside.

Emily didn't like this new, aloof version of Seth, but it was best this way. Or so she tried to tell herself. Her heart didn't buy it.

And with Taylor mad at her… This had not been a good afternoon. Wishing she could make amends with the girl, and aching for the warm man she knew and cared for, she locked the door behind him.

Chapter Nineteen

Seth was about to head to a Friday afternoon appointment with a new rancher client when his cell phone signaled a call from The Wagging Tail. Frowning, he picked up. "Hey, Emily. Listen, I'm booked up this afternoon, but if it's an emergency, I could come this evening. Or first thing tomorrow."

Thanks to the town's healthy grapevine, his reputation was growing. This past week his schedule had been full nearly every day. Even better, he already had appointments set for the following week. If business continued to pick up at the same pace, next month he just might be able to sock away a hefty portion of his earnings for that down payment. "Hey, that website you created for me is working. One of the ranchers asking for an appointment found me that way."

"I like hearing that. Thanks for letting me know."

She sounded as removed and businesslike as him. How had they gotten here?

"Is this about a new dog, or has one of the other animals taken sick?" he asked.

"Neither, so you don't need to come over. I wanted to tell you about Taylor."

Seth groaned. "What'd she do this time?"

"This is actually good news. She's not mad at me anymore, and guess why?" Emily didn't pause long enough for him to come up with anything. "Remember the new dog you stopped by to examine Monday night? Taylor is here now, visiting him. She asked to sit with him after school every afternoon. That's okay with me, but I told her I needed to check with you."

"I'm fine with it." He'd have to pick her up every day, which would be a pain. If business hadn't improved and things between him and Emily weren't so strained, he wouldn't mind so much, but now... "I probably won't be able to pick her up until around dinner time."

"She says she'll walk back to Trenton and catch the after-school-activities bus, so you'll only have to come get her on Thursdays."

"Now that I'm getting busy, that's a relief."

"I think she's ready for a dog."

"Good to know." Seth wasn't going to say anything else before he disconnected, but he wanted Emily's input on something. "Yesterday she asked if anything had come for her in the mail. She's never cared before."

"Is she expecting a package from one of her San Diego friends?"

"She wouldn't say, but I could tell she was hiding something. I get the feeling that whatever she's up to, she knows I won't approve."

"I have no idea what it could be."

"If you find out anything, let me know."

"I doubt she trusts me enough to confide in me again," Emily said.

"But if she does..."

"I can't promise. I don't want to let her down by running to you every time she talks to me. From now on, I'm going to tell her up front when I hear something I think you need to know. She may get mad but at least she'll know I'm being direct with her."

"That makes sense," Seth said, admiring Emily for her straightforwardness. A long pause ticked by, ended by him. "I should go."

"I hope you're still coming to the fund-raiser Saturday night," Emily said.

"I said I'd be there, and I will."

To his own ears he sounded testy. He felt like crap. He missed the easiness he and Emily had shared not that long ago. Until things changed between them, he hadn't realized how much he enjoyed talking with her, how she filled in the gaps in his life.

Tough noogies, buddy. She's moved on.

"I'll let Taylor know that you've okayed her to visit the dog any afternoon she likes," Emily said.

"Don't work too hard." That sounded lame, but was the best he could do.

Scowling at the world, he disconnected.

TODAY WAS WEDNESDAY, the third day in a row that Taylor had visited Paint. Emily didn't allow anyone to name any of the dogs, but this one had a splash of black on his back, just above his tail, that reminded Taylor of a paint stain she'd once gotten on her favorite shirt. She couldn't call him Paint Stain, but Paint worked.

"It's our secret," she confided in a quiet voice.

As softly as she'd spoken, Paint and the five other dogs in the room all perked up their ears. Taylor liked spending time with them without other people around. They let her know right away if they liked her or not. No phony smiles or pretending they were friends until they got a boyfriend.

Not wanting to think about Cat, who she would never, ever be friends with again, Taylor turned her attention to the abused dog a few feet away.

He was still nervous and wouldn't let her come near without baring his teeth and growling. But if she did what Emily advised and stayed quiet, he let her inch a little closer.

Taylor wasn't mad at Emily anymore, especially now. She'd said Paint wouldn't let anyone else do that, and that he was starting to trust Taylor.

Knowing that made it easier for her to get through the

lonely days and wait for the letter from Kayla and Hanna. They were trying to scrounge up the money she needed, and trying to figure out how she could stay with one or the other without telling their parents, who would contact Seth.

But now, Taylor didn't want to leave Paint. Maybe she'd take him with her. Did they allow dogs on Greyhound buses? She'd have to find out.

The problem was, he wasn't ready to go anywhere, and Taylor planned to leave on Monday. The fund-raiser was Saturday night, and she didn't want to miss that. She couldn't leave Sunday without Seth knowing. But Monday, while he was working, she would skip school, head for the bus station and go.

Things between her and Seth were better now, and he was bound to be upset. Taylor felt bad about that, so bad that she wondered if she should stay in Prosperity, after all.

But, no. He'd left her when she was nine. Now he'd find out how rotten that felt. Because believing that her mom had lied, had done what Seth said and taken her away from him when he'd wanted to stay in her life, was too painful to imagine.

She just wished Kayla and Hanna would hurry up and send the money.

THURSDAY AFTERNOON MRS. OAKES was out, running an errand for the upcoming fund-raiser. Emily was sitting at the front desk when Taylor arrived. "Can I sit with Pa— the new dog—for community service today?" she asked.

"You can certainly do that later—if there's time," Emily said. "Today I need you and Cat to work on a few last-minute things for the big event."

Taylor gave her a murderous look. "But I hate working with her!"

Out of sorts thanks to sleep deprivation—the final push to get everything ready for the fund-raiser was exhausting— but also because she missed Seth, Emily frowned. "This thing with you and Cat has gone on long enough. It's time to make up."

"Like that'll ever happen."

"It will if you apologize to her."

Taylor's lips thinned. "Why should I? She's the one in the wrong."

Not about to take sides, Emily nodded. "I understand, but someone has to make the first move."

"It won't be Cat. She doesn't care if we're friends or not."

"I disagree," Emily said. "I'm sure she feels as bad as—"

The bell above the door jingled, and the girl herself stepped inside.

Instantly, the atmosphere turned tense and uncomfortable. Neither girl acknowledged the other. Swallowing the urge to snap at them both to end the feud right now, Emily directed them to pack up boxes she needed to take to the community center downtown, the space she'd reserved for the event.

Before going to tie up a few loose ends, she left them with one last comment. "The fund-raiser is in two days," she said. "It would make me very happy if you made up before then."

"I STOPPED AT home for lunch today," Seth told Taylor as she buckled herself into the pickup after community service. "A letter came for you."

"Where is it? Give it to me!"

She was way too eager. What was in the thing? Seth frowned. "I left it on the kitchen counter. Who's Kayla?"

"How do you know it's from Kayla?" Paling noticeably, Taylor gave him a stricken look. "You opened it, didn't you?"

"For the millionth time, I don't snoop through your stuff. I saw her name on the return address. Who is she?"

"A friend from home."

"San Diego isn't your home anymore."

"Whatever."

"I thought you texted or went on FaceTime with your friends from San Diego."

"I do. All the time."

"Then why would she send a letter?"

Taylor didn't answer. "Emily says Cat and I should make up," she stated, changing the subject.

Now he knew for sure that she was hiding something. *Teenage girls and their secrets.* For now, he let it go. "Are you going to do it?" he asked.

"Not unless Cat apologizes."

"You could make the first move."

Taylor rolled her eyes. "You sound exactly like Emily."

Emily. She filled Seth's every waking thought. Keeping his distance sucked. He wasn't ready to give up on their relationship, if that was what you called it. Once she'd put the fund-raiser behind her and had more time, she just might change her mind and decide she wanted to see him outside the shelter. Seth was counting on that, and intended to do whatever he could to rekindle her interest.

The thought perked up his flagging spirits. He decided to share what he'd been mulling over since Emily had first suggested it. "I've been thinking," he said.

"Uh-oh." Taylor reached for her earbuds.

"For once, will you just listen?"

With a wary expression, she folded her hands in her lap.

"I think we should get a dog," he said.

Her eyes widened and her jaw dropped almost comically. "You mean it?"

He nodded.

"That'd be epic! How about Paint—the new dog from the shelter? Can we adopt him? Please, Seth?"

He hadn't seen her excited like this since she was a kid, and couldn't stop a smile. "I thought Emily didn't name the dogs at the shelter."

"She doesn't. I named him Paint because of the spot on his back. It looks like a paint stain. He likes his name, too. He likes *me*, Seth. I'm the only one he trusts. Well, he's *starting* to trust me. I'm sure Emily will approve us to adopt him."

Seth agreed, but he wasn't sure about taking in an abused animal. "There are issues that come with adopting a dog like Paint. He has a lot of emotional problems. That means he can't be left alone for long periods. At first, maybe not at all. He's okay at the shelter with the other dogs and volunteers around, but once he has his own family, he's going to need someone with him all the time. You're in school and I'm starting to work more and more. There are only a few months left to save enough away for that down payment, and I need to work as much as possible."

Taylor looked confused. "I don't understand why buying the house is so important to you."

She'd never shown an interest before, and Seth took heart. "Because I want us to have a place we can stay in, something we own, so that we can set down real roots."

She didn't respond, but at least she didn't roll her eyes or make a snide comment. "What if you took him with you on your calls?" she asked.

"Right now, he's pretty skittish. Big farm animals he doesn't know could upset him, and vice versa."

"At least think about it?"

She was almost begging, making her request difficult to refuse. "I will."

When they arrived home, Taylor was so revved up over the idea of getting a dog that she stuffed the letter in her backpack with barely a glance at it. She even offered to help with dinner, and chattered about Paint and the fundraiser like a normal kid. Seth couldn't help but feel pleased.

Figuring that whatever was in the envelope couldn't be that important, he enjoyed her upbeat mood while it lasted.

Chapter Twenty

This is it, Emily told herself as she glanced around the Prosperity Community Center auditorium. The night of the fund-raiser had finally arrived. She was ready with a slide show she'd spent hours putting together. The montage featured many of the dogs that had come and gone, and was sure to elicit tears—and prod people to open their wallets.

Thanks to several adult and community-service volunteers, colorful balloons and streamers spruced up the room, and poster-size photos of adopted dogs and their smiling owners covered two walls. Round, linen-clad tables, and chairs for two hundred people filled part of the large space, with food donated by a local catering service in warmers at several eating stations. In the center of the auditorium, the donation tables with the cards Taylor and Cat had decorated awaited silent bidders.

Now the volunteers who'd set up the room stood ready to lend a hand wherever needed. The rest would arrive soon, with some staying late to help with cleanup.

Among the first guests to arrive were Emily's mom and Bill. They'd returned from their travels yesterday. Emily had spoken with them, but hadn't had a chance to visit. Though bleary-eyed with jet lag, they looked happy.

"I can't believe you're here," she said, after embracing them both.

"We wouldn't miss your fund-raiser." Bill patted his hip pocket. "There's a nice check in here for the shelter."

"Aw, I appreciate that."

Her mother smiled. "The room looks great, and you look beautiful."

Emily had splurged on a new rose-colored, wool dress and burgundy suede pumps that added nearly three inches to her height. "Thanks," she said. "I feel so tall."

"You look like a runway model. Bill and I can't wait to tell you about our trip."

Emily didn't have a chance to reply before a group streamed inside. "Excuse me," she said. "I'll call you tomorrow."

As more guests came in, she made sure to say hello and introduce herself to those she hadn't met.

Cat and her parents arrived. After greeting Emily, they headed for the donation tables to look over the items.

Less than five minutes later, Taylor and Seth sauntered through the door. In a sports coat, crisply pressed shirt open at the collar, dress pants and polished shoes, he was irresistibly handsome. But then, he was just as attractive in a flannel shirt and jeans.

Lately, things had been so strained between them. His coming tonight meant a great deal to Emily, and her smile was genuine. To her relief, he offered a smile of his own. That and the appreciative look in his eyes as they darted over her melted parts inside her she hadn't realized were frozen.

"You look beautiful," he said.

"Thank you."

Their gazes caught and held, and her heart almost lifted from her chest. Forget about falling for Seth—she was already there, totally gone, head over heels as she'd never been before. She was in for a lot of heartache, but there was nothing she could do about that but weather through it.

Glancing away, she shifted her attention to Taylor, who for some reason radiated excitement. Which was odd, given that she and Cat were still mad at each other.

"Cool outfit, Emily."

"Thanks, Taylor. I like yours, too. I've never seen you in a dress before."

The girl blushed. "I know, but Seth dressed up, so I did, too. I need to talk to you about that dog I've been sitting with every afternoon."

"I'm a little distracted right now," Emily said. "Can we save the conversation until later?"

"Okay." Taylor glanced across the room, where Cat was standing with a group of adults and teens. "I, um, I need to talk to Cat."

Chin up, she headed toward her friend, who bit her lip and stepped away from the others around her.

"That looks promising," Emily said.

Seth nodded. "I told her she shouldn't run away from her problems. Maybe for once, she listened."

"We'll find out." Resisting the urge to rest a reassuring hand on his biceps, Emily clasped her hands at her waist.

"I should warn you that she has her heart set on adopting that new dog. She already named him."

"You're kidding," Emily said. "Thanks for the heads-up."

Before they could talk further, Bridget, Monica and Bart joined them.

After greeting the two women and meeting Bart, Seth stepped away. "I should go and find Taylor," he said.

"I could watch that man move forever," Bridget murmured as he strode across the room.

Emily's nod elicited a sympathetic look from Monica. "Well, well—I think someone in this room finally took the plunge into the pool of love. When you recover from tonight, call me with details."

Sly, Lana, Dani and Nick showed up next, Dani looking cute in a ponytail and loose wool dress that revealed the tiniest baby bump.

"I'm so glad you're here," Emily told them. "Seth and Taylor are somewhere. Help yourselves to food, and please check out the wonderful donated items and services available for your bid. Sly and Lana, there's a great photo of you and your kids with Brownie over there on the wall."

In what seemed like mere minutes, Mrs. Oakes signaled Emily and pointed at the wall clock. It was time to kick off the evening with a welcome speech. She moved to the front of the room.

"THIS IS SUSANNAH," Emily said, as a slide of the animal filled the screen. "When she first arrived, she was skin and bones, with her left foreleg so damaged it needed amputating. She was also filthy, and crawling with fleas. But she looked at me with those eyes and I was a goner. It's been almost four years since I adopted her, and we've seen each other through some rough times. But no matter what, she's never let me down. That's one reason why I fight for the dogs at the shelter—they love us unconditionally. In return, all they ask for is for us to love them back, give them a safe place to live, and feed and care for them."

Seth couldn't take his eyes off her, and by the silence in the room, others were equally captivated. In elegant heels and a dark pink dress that clung to her slender body and showed off her great legs, she looked spectacular. Her passion for dogs and the shelter was obvious, and her slideshow and accompanying dialogue mesmerizing. A few times he found himself swallowing hard with feeling. Before long Emily's mom and Bill, who were at his table along with Sly, Lana, Dani and Nick, joined everyone else in the room, sniffling and swiping their eyes. Seth knew they'd all give what they could to keep the shelter running.

He was so proud of Emily. He missed her a lot. Tonight looked to be a big success. If only they could celebrate together at the end of the evening…

Taylor and the other high school volunteers had their own table. Seth was relieved to see her and Cat sitting next to each other. From time to time, they bent their heads together, whispering over something. Apparently, they'd made up.

Emily's speech ended. She encouraged her guests to continue enjoying the food, but also to put in their bids.

Seth finished his meal. Between the positive changes in Taylor and the upswing in his patient load, life was looking up. Except for one part of it—the part that included Emily.

Across the room, sitting at a table with some of her bigger donors, she laughed. He couldn't help smiling. She was something special, and without a doubt, the most beautiful women he'd ever known.

Warmth and tenderness he barely recognized flowed into his chest. For nearly two decades, he'd walled himself off from deep feelings. Yet now his heart was wide open and filled to the brim. Wonder of all wonders—with love.

He loved Emily.

When had that happened? He sat back hard in his seat.

"You okay, little brother?" Sly asked.

Dumbfounded, he managed a nod. "Thinking about what to bid on."

"You'd better get over to the tables now, before the bidding closes."

Seth was about to do just that when Bill stood. "My wife and I are dead on our feet. We're going home. It was good meeting you all, and good talking with you, Seth."

"Thanks for all you do at the shelter," Emily's mother added. "Maybe we'll see you again sometime." The couple left.

Seth liked them. Deep in thought, he headed for the donation tables. And realized that he'd actually fallen for Emily around the time he'd met her. He just hadn't admitted it to himself until now.

He loved her. Still staggered by the knowledge, he shook his head again.

What was he going to do about it?

While he looked over the silent-auction items and mulled

over the question, a rancher he'd helped a few days earlier asked for advice about a certain blend of cattle feed. Putting his personal feelings aside, Seth discussed the matter with the man.

Then he put in a bid for a weekend for two at the Prosperity Inn, including breakfast in bed.

At the end of the evening, he and Taylor, along with Cat, her parents and several other teens and parents, stayed to help Emily clean up.

"I've never been to a fund-raiser before," Taylor said. "It was so cool. Did you raise enough money, Emily?"

"It looks that way, but I won't know until we tally up the totals. I'll send out an email on Monday. You were all such a big help with this event. I can't thank you enough. And you two—" she smiled at Taylor and Cat "—you finally made up."

The girls smiled at each other. "We did," Taylor said.

Cat nodded. "Taylor's my best friend, and even if I have a boyfriend, she's really important to me."

Taylor beamed.

"Is it okay if she comes to my house tonight, Seth? This time we're going to have the kind of sleepover where just the two of us talk all night."

"Fine with me," Seth said. "As long as you promise to come to our house next time."

"I will."

"You'll need an overnight bag, Taylor," he said. "When we finish here, we'll go home and get it."

"Great." Taylor leaned closer. "What about Paint?" she whispered.

"I haven't had a chance to talk with Emily about that."

"But you're okay with it?"

"If Emily is. She looks a little tired right now, so I'll talk to her about it later." Along with a few other things.

"Thank you!" Taylor did something surprising—threw

her arms around him. Right there in front of her peers and Emily.

Emily's smile was heartfelt and joyous. Seth's chest expanded more than he'd ever though possible, and he knew he wanted to see that smile every day for the rest of his life.

Holding nothing back, he grinned at her. But she'd moved away.

ON THE DRIVE to the house to pack her overnight bag, Taylor was all smiles. "I'm so happy about Paint," she said. Then she got quiet, picking at her fingernail. "I need to tell you something."

Uh-oh. He shot her a wary look. "What's that?"

"I was planning to run away, back to San Diego. That's what was in that letter from Kayla and my other best friend there, Hanna. Money for a bus ticket."

Seth's heart stuttered in his chest. Unable to hold his feelings in check, he blurted them out. "If you left again, it'd kill me."

Miracle of miracles, she neither mocked him nor shut him out. "I know. Prosperity is my home now, and I'm going to send the money back. I have to learn to trust you, just like Paint will learn to trust me."

His eyes grew damp and he had to clear his throat. "That's beautiful, honey. I'm awful glad. Why don't you invite Kayla and Hanna to visit? I'll bet they'd like the snow."

Taylor looked thoughtful. "Maybe they can come over winter break." A moment later she gave him a timid, sideways look, her eyes glittering in the darkness. "Um, Seth? Can I tell you something else?"

Liking this new, talkative teen, he nodded. "Shoot."

"It's kind of hard to say." She almost winced.

God only knew what was coming. Seth steeled himself. "No matter what you tell me, I'll still care about you."

After a lengthy hesitation, she sucked in a loud breath and blew it out. "The day my mom died…" She swallowed audibly. "We had a fight at breakfast, and I—" Tears filled her eyes and flooded her voice. "I said some really mean things to her." Now she was openly bawling. "I wish...I wish I could take them back."

Seth hated when females of any age cried. But Taylor was confiding in him when she was in such pain, and he was more awed than scared. He reached over and squeezed her hand. "She knew you didn't mean it," he said gruffly. "Wherever she is now, I'm sure she's forgiven you."

"You can't know that. I feel so guilty. Do you have any tissues?"

"Not on me, but there are some clean rags in the glove box." While Taylor rifled through the compartment, he went on. "Maybe you should talk to a professional who can help you deal with your feelings."

"You mean a therapist?" Taylor blew her nose. "I guess I could."

They arrived home. During the ten minutes Taylor spent packing, Seth made some weighty decisions. Her eyes once again dry and clear, she stowed her overnight bag in the rear seat of the pickup.

Instead of heading for Cat's after he buckled himself in, he stayed in the carport. "I've been thinking."

"You do that a lot."

He chuckled. "I know. When we buy the house this spring, I want to fix it up nice—starting with your bedroom. If you have ideas about what you want it to look like, I'm all ears."

"Cool. I'll think about it. Can we go now?"

"In a sec. What I want to say is too important to talk about while I'm driving." He waited until he had Taylor's full attention before he started. "I've always thought of you as a daughter. Now that you're with me for good, I'd like your okay to make our relationship permanent. I want to adopt you."

Her jaw dropped. "You mean that?"

He nodded. "I figure that as long as we're adopting Paint, you and I may as well adopt each other."

"Okay," she said softly. Thanks to the carport lights, he saw her smile brighten her whole face.

"Yes!" Seth pumped his fist in the air, and Taylor laughed. "Now I'll drive you to Cat's."

"She's adopted, too."

"I remember."

One hurdle crossed, one to go. Now if he could convince Emily to give him a chance... What if she didn't?

As he turned onto Cat's street some minutes later, Taylor shot him a worried glance. "It feels all tense in here. Have you changed your mind about me?"

He hated that she was so insecure, but one step at a time. "No way," he assured her. It'd probably take a while before she truly believed that he would stand by her, no matter what. He made a mental note to contact a therapist tomorrow and set up an appointment for her. "We're stuck with each other for good."

Taylor let out a relieved sigh. "Then what's wrong?"

It was time to take some of his own advice and face his problems instead of running away from them. He started by leveling with her. "You're right, I do have something on my mind. It's about Emily. I realized tonight just how much I care about her. I want to tell her, but I know how you feel about her and me in a relationship."

"Oh, that." Taylor waved her hand breezily. "I changed my mind. It's pretty obvious you sort of belong together. Go for it."

"Yeah?" He couldn't help grinning. "To quote a girl near and dear to my heart, that's epic."

She rolled her eyes, but a smile hovered around her mouth. "When are you planning to tell her?"

"I'm thinking I'll go over there after I drop you off." He pulled up Cat's driveway. "Have a good time."

"I will. Good luck, Seth."

"Thanks." He figured he'd need it.

EMILY STOOD OUTSIDE under the shelter's floodlights, shivering in the cold and waiting for Susannah to do her business. It was late and she was tired, but also elated. "We aced the fund-raiser," she told the dog. "If we did as well as I think we did, we'll definitely be around for another year."

If only Seth was here to celebrate the success… But he would never be part of her life, not the way she wanted.

At last Susannah was ready to go inside. With a sigh, Emily turned toward the door. Her feet hurt, but when she'd walked into the apartment tonight, Susannah had begged to go out, and Emily hadn't taken the time to change into comfy shoes.

Someone pulled into the driveway, and the dog began to bark. Emily recognized Seth's truck. Her heart pounding, she froze.

What was he doing here? She'd seen him an hour ago. He wouldn't just drop by, not anymore. Something must have happened. But wouldn't he have called instead? Maybe he had. She'd left her phone upstairs.

Tugging at her leash, Susannah woofed and wagged her tail in a frenzy of excitement.

In what seemed a blink of time, Seth was out of his vehicle and striding toward her. Unable to read his expression, she grew concerned. "Please tell me Taylor's okay."

"Actually, she's fantastic." He greeted Susannah with a pat and a dog biscuit, and then rubbed his hands together. "It's freezing out here. Let's go inside."

Curious what he wanted at this hour, and fearing that he'd decided to resign despite assuring her otherwise and was backing out of his promise like the other men she'd cared about, she nodded somberly. She'd left her apartment door open, and as soon as she unleashed Susannah, the dog hop-limped up the stairs to her doggy bed.

"Going to invite me up?" Seth asked.

Not wanting to hear the bad news in her apartment, Emily shook her head. "Whatever you have to say can be said right here."

"Suit yourself. It's about us."

Emily didn't understand. There was no *us*. "You don't have to worry, Seth," she said, hugging her waist. "First thing tomorrow, I'll start looking for a veterinarian to replace you."

He frowned. "Why would you do that?"

Okay, so maybe he meant to live up to his promise. Deep down, she'd known that, and felt a little guilty for thinking otherwise. Seth wasn't like the other men she'd loved and lost. Once he made a promise, he kept it. Which made him pretty darned special. One of the many reasons she loved him.

On the other hand, if she wanted to get over him, he had to go. "I'm giving you an out," she said.

"I don't want it. Let's sit down."

As bad as Emily's feet hurt, she was too nervous to sit. She remained standing, and so did Seth.

"Watching you work that room tonight..." He shook his head. "You knocked my socks off. If you don't make a ton of money off the fund-raiser, I'll be shocked."

"From your mouth to God's ears." Cocking her eyebrows, she waited for him to say whatever it was that had brought him here.

"You..." Seth broke off, as if searching for the right words. "You're an amazing, beautiful woman, with a heart to match. I'd be a damn fool to let you slip away."

Confused, she stared at him. "I don't understand."

"Let me explain. Years ago, when I lived at my uncle George's, I put a wall around my feelings. I had to. But getting to know you...the wall began to crumble. Stubborn bastard that I am, I fought to keep it intact. I failed." He looked remarkably cheerful about that. "What I'm trying to say is…" He sucked in an audible breath, then exhaled. "I'm, that is, I love you, Emily." His voice cracked with feeling.

Certain she'd misheard, she gaped at him. "No, you don't. You're too busy for love."

"That's what I told myself. Turns out that I was wrong. These past few weeks have been rough, and not just because of the stuff with Taylor. I've missed you, and I want you in my life. Now that the fund-raiser is over and you have more time, is there any chance for us?"

"You're saying that you want a long-term relationship with me?"

"That's exactly what I'm saying."

Could she let her defenses down and take the risk? Trust that he wouldn't leave her? She abruptly sat down. "No way."

His face fell and he joined her on the couch. "I can't accept that. You can turn me down a dozen times and I still won't give up. If it's more comfortable for you, we'll take a step back and move more slowly. Let me take you out to dinner tomorrow night—just dinner. No sex."

That he would do that for her… He was such a good man, and she loved him so much. "Oh, Seth." Her eyes welled up.

"Please don't cry," he said, looking stricken and catching hold of her hands. "All I ask is that you give me another chance."

The warm, caring man searching her eyes was everything she wanted. If he wasn't worth taking a risk for, who was? Smiling through her tears, she silently entrusted him with her heart. "Silly man, I'm crying because I'm happy. I love you, too."

"You mean it?"

She nodded and started to say more, but he stopped her with a kiss. Her thoughts faded away, and for a long time there were no words at all.

Eventually, they broke apart and he rested his forehead against hers. "I've been a real knucklehead."

"I haven't been much better. I was afraid to fall in love. But I'm not scared anymore."

"Now I feel like I just won the lottery."

He kissed the sensitive part of her palm, right at the base of her wrist, and she melted. There was only one problem.

"What about Taylor?" she said. "We both know how she feels about us being together. I don't want her to be upset."

"We talked about that earlier, when I told her I had feelings for you. She said I should go after you."

"She did, huh?"

"Yep." He grinned. "We talked about other things, too. She finally accepted that Prosperity is her home, and she agreed to start therapy. Even better, since we're going to adopt that dog she wants, I suggested that she let me adopt her, as well. She thinks that's epic."

He looked so pleased that Emily laughed. "That's amazing."

He caught hold of her hands again. "Think you can handle a teenage daughter?"

She gaped at him. "Is this a marriage proposal?"

He nodded. "I can't imagine living my life without you."

Emily had to pinch herself to make sure she wasn't dreaming. "Yes, Seth Pettit, I'll marry you."

His entire body relaxed in relief, and his eyes grew suspiciously bright. He swallowed audibly. "I love you, Emily."

"Me, too."

He kissed her again, until she was breathless. Then he pulled back.

"Tonight I bid on that weekend for two at the Prosperity Inn. Even if mine isn't the top bid, we should go in and celebrate. Taylor won't mind—she can stay at Cat's."

"That sounds wonderful. Do you want more kids, Seth? Because at some point, I'd like to have a baby with you."

"Having a little Emily running around, chasing the dogs and bugging Taylor, sounds great to me."

Emily was elated. "Once we're married, do you think Taylor would mind if I adopted her, too?" Emily asked.

Seth thought that was a fine idea.

"There is one more thing," he said. "Once I buy the rental house, it'll take me a year or three to fix it up. Can you live in the midst of a construction project?"

"I could live in a quarantine hut with you and be happy," she teased.

He chuckled, a sound she knew she'd never tire of hearing.

"You never fail to make me laugh." Seconds later, he sobered. "I want to show you just how much I love you, but not on this lumpy couch."

"Then let's go upstairs." Filled with trust and joy for the man she loved, Emily led the way to her apartment.

* * * * *

MILLS & BOON®

Need more New Year reading?

We've got just the thing for you!
We're giving you 10% off your next eBook or
paperback book purchase on the Mills & Boon
website. So hurry, visit the website today and type
SAVE10 in at the checkout for your exclusive

10% DISCOUNT

www.millsandboon.co.uk/save10

0115_PROMO

MILLS & BOON®

Cherish™

EXPERIENCE THE ULTIMATE RUSH OF FALLING IN LOVE

A sneak peek at next month's titles...

In stores from 16th January 2015:

- **Best Friend to Wife and Mother?** – Caroline Anderson
  and **Marry Me, Mackenzie!** – Joanna Sims

- **Her Brooding Italian Boss** – Susan Meier
  and **Fortune's Little Heartbreaker** – Cindy Kirk

In stores from 6th February 2015:

- **The Daddy Wish** – Brenda Harlen
  and **The Heiress's Secret Baby** – Jessica Gilmore

- **A Pregnancy, a Party & a Proposal** – Teresa Carpenter
  and **The Fireman's Ready-Made Family** – Jules Bennett

0115/23